A Darkened Room

Dale T. Phillips

Copyright © 2019 Genretarium Publishing

Cover Design copyright 2019 Melinda Phillips
Cover Images: Pond5.com

ISBN: 1696462174
ISBN-13: 9781696462174

All rights reserved. With the exception of quotes used in reviews, no portion of this book may be reproduced without written permission from the author.
This is a work of fiction. Names, characters, places, and incidents are used fictitiously. Any resemblance to actual persons, living or dead, or events is coincidental.

Try these other works by Dale T. Phillips

Shadow of the Wendigo (Supernatural Thriller)

The Zack Taylor Mystery Series
A Memory of Grief
A Fall From Grace
A Shadow on the Wall
A Certain Slant of Light
A Sharp Medicine

Story Collections
Fables and Fantasies (Fantasy)
More Fables and Fantasies (Fantasy)
Crooked Paths (Mystery/Crime)
More Crooked Paths (Mystery/Crime)
The Last Crooked Paths (Mystery/Crime)
Strange Tales (Magic Realism, Paranormal)
Apocalypse Tango (Science Fiction)
Halls of Horror (Horror)
Jumble Sale (Different Genres)
The Big Book of Genre Stories (Different Genres)

Non-fiction Career Help
How to Improve Your Interviewing Skills

With Other Authors
Rogue Wave: Best New England Crime Stories 2015
Red Dawn: Best New England Crime Stories 2016
Windward: Best New England Crime Stories 2017
Insanity Tales
Insanity Tales II: The Sense of Fear

Sign up for my newsletter to get special offers
http://www.daletphillips.com

DEDICATION

For Jimmy Loftin, taken too soon, and to his loving family who keep his memory alive

ACKNOWLEDGMENTS

It's a tough game to try and outdo yourself with every book, but that's my goal, making each Zack adventure the best it can be.

A hearty thank you to Vincent Zandri, Karen Salemi, Ursula Wong, and others who took the time and effort to read this work (some multiple times) and offer their suggestions to make it better. And to pro writers Dave Zeltserman and David Daniel, for their continued generosity and support. My thanks extend to everyone who helped to make this book possible.

As always, to my wonderful family: Mindy, Bridget, and Erin, for suffering my solitary profession of writing.

To my dear and supportive friends for making things more enjoyable along life's path.

To all who have helped teach me to write, through their works.

To all those who read other Zack Taylor mysteries and wanted more.

And to you, dear reader, my thanks, for reading this one.

Feel free to contact me and let me know what you thought of the book and what it's about.

A Darkened Room

"...the sunbeam that comes through a round-hole in the shutter of a darkened room where a dead man sits in solitude."

— Nathaniel Hawthorne, *American Notebooks*

Dale T. Phillips

A Darkened Room

CHAPTER 1

Little Sebago Lake, Maine, 1996

The dread that cut through me as I paddled toward the cabin was something I couldn't explain. I was not given to premonitions or glimpses of the future, or I'd have never done most of the terrible things that had caused my life to spiral into wreckage. I was simply looking for a missing man. Yes, I'd been told he was in some kind of trouble, but none of the places I'd checked so far had given me this reactive spike of fear from deep in the lizard-brain.

Setting the two-ended paddle crosswise, I let the kayak drift silently. The lake's surface was as flat and gray as a sheet of metal. The morning mist coming off the water was always a sight I enjoyed, so I didn't think my senses were reacting to that. It was the preternatural stillness, without even the calls of birds. There was no movement, no light from the cabin, no stove smoke of a wood fire, though the weather was cool enough to warrant it.

A smart man would have probably had the good sense to turn around and leave things as they were. The way I was wired, the urge to press on was a powerful itch, because getting involved in the problems of others kept me from drowning in my own.

And truth be told, I'd prepared for some sort of trouble. I'd taken the water route rather than the rough, rocky camp trail to the place. Little Sebago, the Maine lake I was paddling on, provided a handy place to ditch the latex gloves and lock-picks in my pocket if the need arose. The off-road vehicle with a kayak rack that I'd borrowed from my reporter friend J.C. Reed was parked across the lake, the license plate smeared with just enough mud to obscure the numbers. I wore an old ball cap with a visor pulled low, a hooded sweatshirt, and faded jeans, with L.L. Bean boots. There were a few others out this early: a canoeist and two men in fishing boats, but I doubted that if pressed, anyone could provide a useful description of me. As a guy with a criminal record and all-too-frequent brushes with the police, I had to be extra careful when poking around. There were a lot of people on both sides of the law who would love to see me jammed up for any reason.

There was no dock or beach in front of the cabin to speak of, just rocks and a muddy flat, with a little grass and scrub growth stretching up from the water. I stepped out and pulled the kayak up, the noise of the bottom scraping on the earth a loud violation of the stillness. There was no place to tie the kayak off, so I got it far enough up where it wouldn't drift away.

The mud sucked at my boots. It oozed back into place, but a few more steps, and I'd leave tracks if I kept going. At the edge of the scrub, I pulled out a couple of the plastic grocery bags I'd stuffed in the sweatshirt. These went on my feet like booties, and I tied them around my ankles. The latex gloves went on my hands.

I went up onto the small porch that faced the lake. The solid knock I gave on the door sounded loudly, and my call-out echoed back from the mist. No response. I looked through the glass of the door top and the side windows, but it was dark inside, and the one thing I hadn't thought to bring was a flashlight. There was one back in the vehicle, but I wasn't about to paddle over there and back again. I walked a slow, complete circle around the cabin, noting the turned-over canoe off to the side, secured to a tree with a padlocked chain. There was a late-model Ford sedan parked out front. I peered in the windows of the car and tried the doors, but all were locked. In this neck of the Maine woods, people didn't usually lock their cars. I thought about popping the trunk and searching the inside of the vehicle, but I decided to check the cabin first.

The sun struggled to burn away the morning mists as I went back to the porch. I took out my picks and started on the lock, a skill I'd acquired from some people I'd worked with a long time ago. My skills were rudimentary at best, but this simple device was cracked in under a minute.

Inside the cabin, I felt the damp chill that comes with being by the water, and I squinted through the gloom. Then the smell hit me, and my stomach lurched. A ray of sun poked through a hole in the shutter to illuminate the slumped body of a man sitting in a chair. The top of his head was so much shredded flesh, the filthy extinguished remains of a human life. I gulped, and only kept down my breakfast by sheer effort of will.

Edging forward, I saw the shotgun on the floor, a haunting reminder of more of my sins. Not long before, I'd plugged a shotgun that I was sure would be used in an attempt on my life, and the result was that an evil woman had blown her face off. Now this scene showed me a similar gory outcome, and I felt the guilt once more crushing me. My head buzzed like it was full of mad wasps, and I stood breathing in and out, trying to process everything. From the remains, I really couldn't tell if the body was Winslow Sprague, the man I'd been looking for, but I'd bet money it was.

My entry had disturbed a moth that now fluttered against the window in a vain attempt to escape. I had a crazy notion that it was the soul of the dead man trying to leave this place of death.

When I could move again, I took a step and heard the floorboard creak beneath me. The sunlight showed more of the interior. Was this a simple suicide? Sprague had been in trouble, so had he taken the quick exit? There was no note, but that was no indication either way. The act itself was the dramatic final note of suicides, so many didn't feel the need to elaborate further.

I didn't like it. His daughter Miriam had indicated he was on the run, hiding from someone because of something he'd done. This was far too convenient. The reason I'd come to Maine in the first place some time ago was that my friend's death was thought a suicide, when it had been a murder staged to look that way. Police didn't investigate much on a closed case of self-inflicted death, and it shut down most of the questions. The death of Winslow Sprague would leave a lot of unanswered issues for me and for his daughter, and I didn't want it to end like this. Doubtless the psychiatrist I'd seen would have said my past influenced what I did next.

There was an easy way to keep the pot boiling. All I had to do was remove the death weapon, and the scene would change to look like a murder. And murders mean open, ongoing investigations. I took out a kerchief and carefully leaned down and picked up the shotgun, all the while knowing I was committing a felony. I gave a final look around, and slipped out the door, locking it behind me.

I went back to the kayak, mud pulling at the bags on my feet. The shotgun went inside the kayak, and I stripped off the gloves and eased the craft back into shallow water. I removed the bags from my feet and swished them around in the lake, then turned them inside out and balled them up. I got in and pushed off against the lake bottom with an end of the paddle.

The mist was now gone, and I felt open and exposed. I stroked at a steady pace, cold sweat popping out on my neck and shoulders and running down my back. About a hundred yards from the cabin, I quickly slipped the shotgun out and pushed it into the water, letting it sink to the bottom. If the police were thorough and dragged the lake at all, they'd do it within throwing distance of the shore of the cabin, but they couldn't and wouldn't drag the whole lake. Unless someone had been watching me in those few seconds, no one would know. At least I hoped.

Back at the other side of the lake, I donned a pair of sunglasses, further hiding my face. I racked the kayak and drove to the main road, then stopped and removed the mud from the license plate. Then I drove back to Portland, feeling a gripping dread all the way.

Dale T. Phillips

A Darkened Room

CHAPTER 2

When I'd left Miami, I'd felt like a ghost for simply passing through and leaving a place with little else but locked-down emotions and few connections. After I'd come to Portland, I'd finally opened up. I'd even fallen in love with Allison, a nurse, who was The One. I thought she could handle the darkness that haunted my life. But the violence and danger was too much for her, and when she'd been injured in one of the attempts on my life, she started drinking, and her life went off the rails. I'd been down a similar path before, and was fighting to not do it again.

J.C. and I finally got her the help she needed. She was diagnosed with PTSD, and a psychiatrist had told me I likely had it as well.

Allison had been smart enough to leave, though it cost her everything. She transformed completely, returning to her earlier life as a painter, and was doing better now. She was off in New Mexico, painting in Taos and living with another artist, a man who wasn't me. She poured her pain and stress onto canvas, like Frida Kahlo, and the truth of her images burned like flame. I was told she seemed happy, and was also getting a bit of fame for her pictures, which were commanding a high price on the art market. Good for her.

Me, I was a hollow shell, a disconnected ghost again, wandering around Portland, seeing the places we'd been and wishing Allison was back with me. Stuck in my own Hell. Not being with her felt like having someone pull barbed wire through my guts. She had grounded me, kept me sane, while everything around me spun into whirlwinds of insanity. The people who had died because of my actions haunted me like Furies, and I staved off the drinking by immersing myself in dangerous situations, risking my life to feel something other than the pain of waking up every day without Allison. I'd been told on more than one occasion I had a death wish.

The ache was so bad that from time to time I tried dating other women to fill the void. There were some who loved the thrill of being with a troubled ex-con. They didn't last long, nor did those who tried to fix me. My violent way of life could be like a virus transmitted to others, and every encounter made me less miserable for a short time, before sinking me further down afterward. None of the women understood where my anger came from, or why I'd wake in the night shivering from the visit of another bad memory. They did not comprehend a life of darkness, of how violence marks a person and infects everything.

My friend J.C. understood this, and kept me busy helping people out. He knew many good folks and lost souls who had problems. Sometimes it was a simple matter, like moving furniture or chopping firewood for someone who was sick or had been injured. Splitting a pile of wood piece by piece with an axe is very therapeutic for someone like me. I'd taken on a mission in life to help others, but it was the only method I knew to keep occupied enough to keep all my own ghosts at bay. By focusing on someone else, I wouldn't dwell on my own self-pity and demons.

Most people didn't have the wherewithal to stand up to someone who was bullying them, but that was my meat and drink. I took on the title of Security Consultant, and got paid for a variety of odd gigs. I didn't mind sticking my nose in where it didn't belong, even when it got punched as a result. That usually gave me an excuse to punch back, to use my life in the martial arts to smash my frustration and rage out on someone who deserved it.

But as I was aging, I was slowing down. Adding that to my series of injuries, I could no longer take the battering of the ring, so I'd stopped competitive kickboxing. Martial arts had helped me focus my problems, but I needed a style with less damage. So I'd begun aikido a few months before, and it was helping a great deal. It was the path of harmony, instead of aggression. I had always met anger with anger, and force with force. Now rather than use powerful strikes and attacks, I was learning how to move to keep someone from hurting me. Aikido is a way of moving meditation, and advanced aikido practitioners were calm, serene people, exuding peace.

I desperately needed some peace, because my actions had got me into a lot of trouble, and the local police were not my biggest fans. I only stayed out of jail by retaining Gordon Parker, the best criminal attorney north of Boston. His fees were exorbitant, and the only reason I could pay them was because in some of the situations I'd been in, I'd been able to relieve some bad people of healthy stashes of ill-gotten gain. Whatever was left over I put to doing some good. My dead friend Ben, the reason I'd come to Maine, would have said it was a way of assuaging my conscience.

So this latest mess was a result of J.C. introducing me to one more person who needed help, a woman named Miriam Sprague, who'd asked me to look for her missing father. Winslow Sprague had given her hints of trouble from other people. She didn't know exactly what it was, but had been worried when her father had stopped answering her calls. She'd given me a list of places he might go. I'd been looking for several days when I finally went to the cabin and found him. Or what had been him.

As soon as the body was found, the police would talk to Miriam. The moment my name came up, they'd be grilling me like a salmon for my involvement. I'd been tangled up in too many homicides in the Portland area, and law enforcement on several levels was itching for an excuse to lock me up. My taking the shotgun from the crime scene was worse than stupid, but there was nothing I could do about it now. I hadn't told Miriam what I'd found, and kept looking, going to places Sprague had been and asking if anyone had seen him. Nothing I had encountered since hinted at what had happened to him. But he must have run into something, and I was determined to find out what, if only to give the police something other than my own hide for their trophy case.

Maybe it was cruel to not tell Miriam, but to do so would have ended my freedom forever. So I was selfish as well as stupid. But I was already in more hot water than I might be able to get out of.

I began working on my alibi.

CHAPTER 3

Outside my apartment, Sergeant LaGasse of the Portland PD was leaning on his standard cop-car Crown Vic, and when he saw me, he crooked a finger. He wasn't tall, and rounder and softer than he should have been. I noticed he was still chewing toothpicks, the habit that had replaced smoking. When I first came to town, I'd shaken things up and made his life a lot more complicated. I kept finding bodies, and I got the distinct feeling he'd prefer I be one of the dead ones to turn up.

He took out the toothpick. "Lieutenant McClaren wants to see you."

"And he sent you? What did you do to piss him off?"

His shook his head. "Always with the funny stuff. Get in. And be glad you're not riding in the back in cuffs."

That was the end of our conversation, all the way to the station. All he saw when he looked at me was my prison record, and all I saw was an over-the-hill cop who no longer took chances or looked beyond the painfully obvious. He seemed to be looking forward to doing even less when he retired. He should have been working real cases, not being a taxi service to bring me in. A phone call would have done that.

Of course we went to an interrogation room. LaGasse crossed his arms and leaned on a wall. Lieutenant McClaren was seated, with a folder on the table in front of him. I took the chair opposite, sensing there was someone watching us through the one-way mirror. McClaren was a tall, sunburned, rangy guy who looked like he should be in the outdoors, not dwelling among the offices. He was a hard-nosed professional, and though we'd tangled, we respected each other. He was a fair man, and had never harassed me more than his job demanded, unless pressured from above. That didn't mean he was any less a cop when I was involved in a crime.

"Lieutenant. How have you been?"

He skipped the pleasantries. "You were looking for Winslow Sprague."

I feigned surprise. "Yeah, for about five days now. Haven't found him yet." I frowned. "Wait a minute. *Were* looking?"

McClaren didn't reply, but opened the folder, took out a photo, and pushed it towards me. It was an 8-by-10 color glossy of Sprague's dead body, missing the top of his head. I made a sound in my throat and pushed it away.

"Jesus, Lieutenant. You could have warned me." I hoped I'd shown enough surprise.

"Does he look familiar?"

"He doesn't look anything like the pictures I have, if that's him." I gave the photo some side-eye. "What happened?"

"Looks like a shotgun."

He said nothing more, watching me. Old cop trick. I decided to play along for the benefit of the hidden audience.

I nodded. "If it was a suicide, you wouldn't be grilling me like this."

He pushed over a yellow legal pad and a pen. "Retrace your steps from the time you got involved to last night."

"Why? I didn't kill him."

"Maybe not, but a lot of people are tired of seeing you mixed up in so many homicides."

I scratched my head. "What is it you're looking for? Where I went, who did I talk to? I'm a bit fuzzy on some details."

"Best as you can."

"Since you asked so nicely." I began writing, starting with my introduction to Sprague's daughter Miriam. To give me plausible denial, I shifted the timeline a bit, omitting my visit to the cabin. No one spoke, not even the ever-snarky LaGasse. Either he'd mellowed, or he was on a short leash. It must be somebody important on the other side of the mirror. I finished and passed it to McClaren, who scanned it.

"Why did Sprague's daughter come to you?"

"I help people."

LaGasse coughed.

I ignored him and went on. "J.C. heard she had a problem, and called me."

"We've been down this road. You don't have a license to do P.I. work."

"No, but I do have a license from the city as a Security Consultant." I took out one of my business cards and tossed it on the table. McClaren ignored it. I shrugged. "If I'd found him, I might have been able to keep this from happening."

LaGasse let fly with a hoarse guffaw. "You suck at that as bad as you do being a straight civilian."

I turned to look at him, my control slipping away. "Can you actually remember a long time ago, back when you might have been a good cop, instead of just a useless hack on the payroll, counting the days until retirement?"

The jibe hit home, and LaGasse's face sagged as if I'd gut-punched him. He probably would have lunged at me, but McClaren gave him a glare that would melt glass.

I realized several things. One, yes, there was someone, or a number of someones behind the mirror, and this was a little bit of theater. McClaren was demonstrating for the onlookers that he was being tough on me, as he'd been instructed. LaGasse was here because he always got under my skin, and an angry person will sometimes lose control and say something they shouldn't. But McClaren knew I could dish it out as well, so maybe LaGasse was also here as some kind of punishment. Maybe McClaren felt the same way about a cop who no longer tried very hard.

I breathed in and out slowly, getting the control back. I had to keep my head. I waved my hand at the picture, as if shooing it away. "Any idea who did it?"

"When we find out, you can read it in the papers. Meanwhile, keep your trouble-causing ass out of this."

"His daughter wanted him found, you found him. That's the end of my part."

"It damn well better be. None of your shit of kicking around, stirring things up. There's an arrest warrant for obstruction of justice all ready to go, just waiting to have your name filled in. One step over the line, and we'll drop the hammer on you. Understand?"

I frowned. "You know I don't respond well to threats."

"Tough shit. There's a lot of pressure to can your ass. You've used up all your get-out-of-jail-free passes, and state and federal people are panting to put you through a legal wood-chipper. You're a sixteen-point buck, and it's hunting season. So take a vacation or go find a hole until we get this taken care of."

I stood up, my anger once more seeping out. "You get the hell off my back. Do your job and find out who did this."

On TV or in the movies, a cop in his role would have said something like *"Bet on it!"* Truth is, sometimes the police catch a killer, and sometimes not, no telling in advance. McClaren didn't make empty promises, or empty threats, for that matter. So I knew he

A Darkened Room

was getting pressured to come down on me, and I had no doubt the forces of the law were gearing up to put me in a wringer.

Same story, different death.

Dale T. Phillips

CHAPTER 4

Emerging from the police station, I rubbed my eyes with the heels of my hands. Idiot that I was, I'd plunged into serious trouble again. I'd been making significant progress at getting myself under control, but my stupid impulsive action with the shotgun might jeopardize everything. The cops were panting after me like hounds on the scent, but to tell the truth, there was no way I could stay away from this one. I'd been hired to find the guy, only to discover his body. I hoped the cops could track down the killer or killers. If not, I'd have to do something about it.

Miriam lived alone in a small house on Walton Street, just off Forest Avenue, not far from where I was. The police would have informed her by now. I doubted she'd be at her job at a semiconductor plant out in South Portland, so I called J.C. with the news, and took a cab to go see her.

She answered the door with red, puffy eyes. No surprise that she'd been crying. She was medium height, with frizzy brown hair.

"I'm so sorry," I said.

She held a tissue to her face and stepped back, and I entered at the invitation.

Two men in suits were sitting in her living room, glaring at me.

I nodded my head. "Who are they?"

"Police. They have some questions about Dad."

I looked them over. "They the ones who told you about finding him?"

"No, another two were here earlier. I have their card."

I frowned. "Can I see it?"

Miriam went to the kitchen, while the two men bent their heads close together and whispered, giving me sidelong glances. I was getting a strange vibe.

"Here it is."

I took the card and nodded at the name on it, one of the detectives I knew from my police encounters. "Did they ask you anything?"

"They tried, but I was a little shaken. I told them to come back later."

"How long ago was that?"

"About two hours."

I tapped the card on my other hand. "So now a different pair is here. That's kind of odd."

"Is it? Maybe the other two got busy."

"Maybe." I looked at them. "Did they show you badges?"

"They flashed some ID, but I wasn't looking very closely, I'm afraid."

Interesting. I took a few steps in. "Guys, could I have a word with you? Outside?"

They looked at me and scowled. I smiled. "It's kind of important."

They looked very reluctant to do it. They rose slowly, keeping their gaze on me the whole time. I opened the door and held it for them, gesturing for them to go ahead of me.

Miriam looked puzzled. "What is it?"

"I just want to check something out. Won't take a minute."

I stepped out to the sidewalk with the pair. One had slicked-back black hair, was tall and lanky, with long arms poking from his sleeves and showing a lot of wrist. The other had brown hair and was two inches shorter, but wider and more solid. They both had shoulder holsters under their suit jackets.

I looked from one to the other, committing their faces to memory. "So who the hell are you?"

They looked at each other. The tall one spoke. "Police."

"Police my ass. I know all the Portland detectives, and I've never seen you two."

The tall one showed some teeth in what might have been a stylized smile. "We're FBI, actually. Didn't want to scare her. Who are you?"

"Now I know you're not cops, or you'd know who I am." I'd been involved in so much in the last couple of years, and all the cases had garnered a ton of very unwanted publicity. "Can I see some ID?"

"What's your interest in this?"

"Show me valid ID, and we'll have a nice chat. Who are you guys working for?"

The tall one leaned in. "You don't want to fuck with us, cowboy."

"Actually, I do. Kind of how I operate."

The tall one nodded his head toward his partner, who grinned and stepped in close. He snapped a punch at my face, but I stepped back, and all he caught was air. He scowled and lunged, but my shot caught his gut first. It felt like hitting a heavy bag. He grunted and stepped back. That punch would have dropped a man lesser trained. His partner already had his gun out, down at his side.

A vehicle rolled by behind them on the street, and J.C. honked his horn. I waved, never taking my gaze off the pair.

The tall one nodded. "Another time, then. Maybe a place not so public. You will not be so lucky."

He tapped the gun against his side, and they moved away. I got my breathing under control. I stood there until J.C. came up.

"Friends of yours?"

Dale T. Phillips

CHAPTER 5

When J.C. joined me inside, Miriam looked confused. "What was that all about? Where did they go?"

"Those weren't cops, Miriam."

"Then who were they? And why did they want to know about my father?"

"I don't know. But they're dangerous."

She ran her hands through her hair. "I don't know what is going on."

I let J.C. comfort her. I wasn't good at that sort of thing, and he was. After a few minutes he got her back on an even keel.

We sat in the living room, and Miriam looked at me. "How did you find out about my dad?"

"The cops told me when they brought me in."

"Brought you in?" Miriam frowned. "What for?"

"To ask about my ties with your father. Since it's not an accident, they zeroed in on me." I'd almost used the word suicide, but was glad I hadn't. "Because I'd been asking around, they found out about it and pulled me in. Because of past events, they are extremely suspicious when my name pops up in connection with any crime."

"But you didn't kill him."

"Much to their dismay."

"They said it happened at his cabin by the lake. Had you been out there?"

"No," I lied. It came easily. Good thing, because I'd have to maintain that alibi. "I was working that list of names and places you gave me, but hadn't got there yet."

She nodded and looked around. "Would anyone like some coffee? I made a fresh pot."

"That would be nice, thank you." J.C. also nodded assent. She left the room.

J.C. had creases on his brow. "So you don't know who those two were?"

"Not a clue. Pros, though, competent strong-arm men. Both packing. Bet you didn't even see the gun he had out."

"Afraid not. I could sense something was wrong, though."

"That's for sure. They were on to Miriam pretty quickly."

"What if they were the ones that did it?"

I shook my head. "Then she's in a lot of danger."

"Did you get anywhere before the police nabbed you?"

"No, I talked to the people Miriam listed. I went to all the Portland locales. No one had seen or spoken to him in some time. Nobody acted like they were lying about it. There didn't seem to be any indication of anything wrong. He was playing it close to the vest, not getting in touch with locals."

Miriam came back with two mugs of coffee. "Well, now the police can handle it, right?"

I exchanged a look with J.C. He gave an almost imperceptible nod, letting me know I was clear to tell her. "Miriam, if it's okay with you, I'm going to keep digging into this."

"Why?"

"The police probably don't have much more than I did to go on. I hope they can find something, but the longer a case goes unsolved, the less likely it is that they catch whoever did it. They'll do what they can, but a suspect doesn't turn up quick, the case gets moved to the back burner, sad to say."

"You mean they stop looking."

"If they don't get any solid leads, yes. They focus on what they can solve. They've only got so much for resources, then they get other cases. Me, I can follow more leads, keep looking."

"I'm taking a leave of absence. I can't pay you for any of that."

"I'm not asking you to. Someone got to him before I could find him. I feel responsible. So it's personal for me, too. I won't stop."

She got up and came over to me and reached down to give me a hug. "Thank you."

I was embarrassed, and looked at J.C. for support. He was looking down into his mug.

She released me, and I went on. "I know this hurts, and we went over this, but I'm going to need more information from you. You thought he was here, so you gave me the local info, but I may need to trace his steps back further."

"Up where he worked?"

"Yes, as much as you can tell me about his life up there."

"The last few months he was only there during the week. Then he'd come down here to Portland for the weekend. Mostly to the cabin."

"Why?"

"To spend more time with me. We'd go out to dinner, do things together. It was nice."

"He hadn't done that before?"

"For so many years, his work was his life. The town's a few hours away. When I moved down here, I didn't see him as much until recently."

"Did he say why he changed routine?"

"He'd been talking about retirement, what he'd do after he left work."

"Did he use that cabin by the lake a lot?"

"That's where he stayed when he came down. I told him he could stay here, but he said he preferred his privacy. All those years up in the woods, I guess. He liked canoeing. He had one there."

I almost slipped and said that I knew. *Damn.*

"I'll go up there. If you give me some names and information, I'll look around, see what I can turn up. Maybe that's where this all started."

Miriam looked out the window. "He worked that job for almost thirty years. I can't imagine something suddenly coming up."

I was quiet. The only thing I could figure was that he was an accountant. They deal with money, so that was the most likely scenario for something big and wrong suddenly occurring.

"How many times did he call you in the last two weeks?"

"Twice. The first time he'd said that he'd run into some problems, so he'd be hard to reach."

"Any indication of what it was?"

"No. Then he called four days ago, said his problems had got worse. Said he loved me, told me to be careful answering the door, don't go to places alone, because he'd got into some trouble, and people might ask about him. I got worried, of course. He'd never spoken to me like that. I called J.C. and asked his advice, and he said to call you."

"Sorry I couldn't have been more effective."

She threw up her hands. "If he wouldn't tell me what was going on, I wouldn't expect you to find out in only three days. This is all so strange. I really want to know what happened, but I can't ask you to involve yourself any further."

J.C. spoke up. "It's therapy for him. Without something like this, he tears himself up."

Miriam looked at me. "Is that true?"

I shrugged. "More or less."

"So this is your hobby, of sorts? Helping people?"

I stared down into my mug. "I have a lot of bad karma to work off."

"So what do we do now?"

"Miriam, I'm going to have my large friend Theo hang around, just in case. He'll keep you safe. Can he stay here in the house?"

"I guess. Do you think that's really necessary, though?"

"I sure hope not."

Dale T. Phillips

CHAPTER 6

Theo was in when I called, and he agreed to stay with Miriam. I paid well, and he was always happy to pick up a little work on the side. The presence of a large, intimidating black man should keep away the wolves, and he even had his own gun. He showed up with an overnight bag, and I made introductions.

J.C. dropped me back at my place. I noticed a woman in a dark suit standing next to my car. She was wearing flats and was about five-eight, trim, and stood in a balanced pose that a lot of athletes, bodyguards, soldiers, and martial arts practitioners have. As I approached, she uncrossed her arms and took off her sunglasses to stare me down. She had long black hair and intense green eyes. She was attractive, even striking, despite a slightly crooked nose that had obviously been broken.

"Zack Taylor." She said it as a statement, not a question. She held up a black leather holder that contained a badge and an ID. "Casey Selkirk, FBI. Can I have a word with you?"

I sighed. Of course she was a fed. A real one. But I'd seen too many, and didn't care much for them. "What the hell do you people want now?"

"Like I said, a word."

"Well *I* want a shower, some rest, and something cool to drink. Some other time, maybe."

She smiled, but it was a look with steel behind it. "I heard you were a hardass. But I need to talk to you, sooner rather than later. We don't have to make this official. But if you want it that way, it's going to take a lot longer."

"Have to warn you that scare tactics aren't particularly effective right now. I've already been threatened by the authorities today. Among others."

"I know."

I studied her. "Ah. That was you behind the mirror at the station."

She gave the merest of nods.

"You couldn't have chimed in then?"

"Our conversation should be a little more private."

"Well, as nice as that might be, I'm not in the mood. I need a shower."

"I don't mind if you smell like a goat. I've got work to do."

"You going to tell me we can do this the hard way or the easy way? Because if you know about me, you know how it's going to be."

Her eyes flashed as if she wanted to give a command, but I saw her take a breath. "Okay, how about a request, then, asking nicely. I'll give you an hour to get cleaned up."

"Damn generous of you."

She shook her head. "Don't be a pain in the ass all your life."

I smiled, a tired thing. "My stock in trade."

She held up a finger. "One hour. And you better be there and answer my knock."

As I cleaned up, I wondered just why the FBI was interested in this case. They were so much worse than local cops. My penchant for trouble might have finally finished me.

When the knock on the door sounded, I looked through the peephole first, because with all the people that wanted to do me harm, it would be idiotic to open the door without checking.

"Agent Selkirk. Come on in."

"Thank you. I appreciate your seeing me."

"And I appreciate your appreciation. Most of the time, I get summoned with an 'or else.' I don't much care for it."

"Well, you do have quite a colorful background."

I made a sound that was halfway between a snort and a grunt. "That's a polite way of saying you think I'm a dirty crook."

"And how would you describe yourself, then?"

"Gentleman adventurer who's run into some bad luck. Like Rick in *Casablanca*."

That got me a brief smile. "Rick, huh? Don't think so. The local and state police want your ass in a sling. There's a biker gang that would love to see your name on a tombstone, so they could piss on it. If the Boston mob wanted to come back up this way, you'd be first on their list of who to get rid of. Who else? Oh yeah, the Yakuza, the remaining Holloway brother, some big-shot land developer, and the Fire Marshal, who swears you're an arsonist. Am I missing anyone?"

"A Treasury agent who thinks I was put here to sabotage his career."

She put her hands up. "Okay, truce."

"Done." I looked around. I knew I wasn't quite set up for entertaining. "Let's sit down. Can I get you anything?"

"No, thank you. This isn't social."

"It never is with you people."

She opened her mouth to retort, then nodded. "Fair enough."

So we sat for a moment. She looked as if she expected me to ask her what this was all about, but I let her go first. A wise man said you learn more by listening than talking.

She plowed right in. "You know more about Winslow Sprague's death than you admitted at the station."

"This again. I told you all what I know."

"You've cooperated with authorities in the past, in exchange for immunity. What if I offered that now?"

"There's nothing I need immunity for."

She sat back, watching me closely. "Do you own a kayak?"

I tried to control myself, but I knew she was likely well-trained, and had picked up on my heart-sinking reaction. "No."

"Borrowed one, then. Where were you yesterday morning?"

"What time?"

"About seven-thirty."

"Sunday. I was sleeping."

"Anybody verify that?"

"Nope. I live alone. As you can see."

She watched me, waiting to see if I would dig myself in with further explanations or questions, like guilty people usually do. But I knew some of the tricks, and kept my mouth shut.

"So now you know *I know* you went there," she went on. "We got a call from a concerned citizen about some dude in a kayak dropping something in the lake, not far from where the body was found in his cabin. For the record, I know you didn't kill Sprague. Lucky you, he'd been dead some time before you went out there."

I just shrugged, not trusting myself to speak.

"But all I had to do at the station was tell them you'd seen the body and didn't report it, and you'd be in a cell now. I don't think even the great Gordon Parker could have sprung you."

Silence.

She went on. "So why am I being so nice, when you're being a self-protecting prick? Because you're scared, I get that, because you were in the wrong place at the wrong time. Nobody else has to know you went out there. It'll be our little secret."

I swallowed. "You seem to be accusing me of something. I'm going to call my attorney."

"The hell you are. You can deny it eight ways to Sunday, but we both know you went out to check out that cabin, and you high-tailed it when you found him. I'm not trying to nail you for the murder, because I know someone else killed him. Anything you tell me now doesn't leave this room, and it's just the two of us. This case is a lot bigger than you, and you're not the one I want. But I have to know everything. Was the shotgun there when you found him?"

My back was to the wall. "My interactions with the feds have not been amicable. I've been lied to before, and lied about, and went to prison for it. Why the hell should I trust you?"

She considered. "If I'd wanted to, I'd have you in a little room right now with a district attorney squeezing your nuts. I gave you the benefit of the doubt, because as I said, you've cooperated in the past. I've seen your file. You're not the master criminal others think you are, so don't worry about Portland PD or the Staties. This thing is big, way bigger than you, and I need every scrap of information I can get. I need honesty, not some frightened little man trying to save his own skin."

Damn, her look was intense. She sure was being frank. And she had a point. I jumped off the cliff. "The shotgun was there."

She let out her breath. "Where is it now? Bottom of the lake?"

I nodded.

"I want it. Can you show me the general area? Best as you can? I'm guessing you weren't stupid enough to have your fingerprints anywhere on it, but it might tell me something about whoever did use it. I've got access to some tracking resources."

"If we go out there with a team and divers, everyone will know I'm really involved."

"Yeah. How about if you and I go out by ourselves, and I'll mark the area. I can come back and say an anonymous tip saw somebody in the area. You're out of it. So grab your gear and let's go for a boat ride."

"I'm putting my life in your hands."

"It's been there since I got on the case, sugar. Let me tell you though, if these people are who I think they are, *I* could be the least of your worries."

CHAPTER 7

"We'll take my ride," she'd said, and when we walked around the corner and I saw it, I knew why. A canoe was strapped to a rack on the top, and tied down. I glanced at her.

"Yup," she said. "One way or the other, you were going out with me today. In cuffs or without. If you'd made me drag the whole lake, I might have tipped you overboard. Cuffed."

I wasn't a hundred percent sure she was joking.

"Glad to help," I said.

"You mean glad to help keep your ass out of jail."

"That too."

As we drove, she opened the conversation. I sure as hell wasn't going to. "Can't quite figure you out," she said. "I'm new to these parts, and everybody with a badge seems to want to pound you like a nail."

I ran a hand through my hair. "My record, of course. Once a con, always a criminal, right?"

"Going by statistics, probably."

"When I came here, I ran into some pretty bad people. When the police came to clean up the mess, they didn't seem to want to sort out the guilty from the not-so-guilty."

"Generally speaking, someone involved in that many deaths and criminal rings is usually one of the sort that's not on the side of the angels." She gave me a sidelong look for a brief second before turning back to the road.

"Someone's got to stop these people. They get away with things for far too long. And I try to keep good people from getting hurt."

"As do I. For the record, I think you've done some good. I also think you owe your freedom to your attorney. He's kept the wolves at bay. I bet that cost you a pretty penny."

"He's worth it."

She gunned the engine to whip around a slow-moving vehicle in front of us, and swerved back in after she'd passed. "I'm kind of surprised that the Treasury guy, what's his name?"

"Fielding."

"That's him. Wonder why he hasn't sicced the IRS on you to dig up where you got the money to pay for those legal fees. Gordon Parker doesn't come cheap."

I said nothing, staring straight ahead, wondering if she was baiting me.

She went on. "I mean, not getting the insurance for your dojo that was burned, that had to hurt. Portland Fire Marshal's not a fan of yours either, apparently. And I haven't noticed any regular job you've held. This security consultant gig you're doing, that paying the bills?"

She knew far too much about my private affairs. I kept my voice even. "This an interrogation?"

She shrugged. "I'm curious. You don't act like a crook, but you've got a hell of a lot of shade around you. So much so I'd think you were really deep undercover, or really involved, like those Mason Carter newspaper stories."

"He uses me as a cash cow to peddle his lies."

"But he's backed off a bit, hasn't he? He used to hammer on you, but I haven't seen your name crop up in months."

"Maybe he had a change of heart."

"Doubt he's got one. You guys make nice?"

I took a deep breath and decided to tell her the truth. "Some white supremacists I tangled with had gone after him. Took him for a ride, threatened and beat him. He gave me a little background that helped me screw them up, hoping I'd go after them. I did."

"I'll say. That was quite a mess. And that Helen Schiller woman, dying on her front porch like that, with her face blown off. Shotgun, too, like this case. Curious."

I sucked my teeth. "We're going to the lake, but you didn't say we were going fishing."

She laughed. Despite the circumstances, I kind of liked it.

"Well, I see these loose ends, and I don't like all the unanswered questions. Your file's thick, but I get the impression it's not thick enough. Treasury man Fielding was one of those after you, and suddenly he backed off as well."

"I gave him a good tip on some art forgeries."

"See, that's what I mean. You're like a one-man crime stopper." Another glance. "And for the record, I didn't agree with them cutting Southern loose, especially knowing he'd go after you. That was a raw deal, and I know it cost you. Sorry, on behalf of the good guys."

Mention of Ollie Southern made my heart rate increase, along with my anger. But I took a few breaths to get control of my emotions. "You've done a lot of digging."

"That's what I do. You weren't the only one looking for Sprague. When your name came up as a person of interest, I took one look at your background and knew there was more to the story. So yeah, I'll be taking you over the hurdles on the real story of you finding the body, but it doesn't go to anyone else, unless you keep shit from me. We'll mark the lake, I'll call it in, and provided we find the gun around there, you could be out of it. And you'll want to be."

"Okay."

"So why'd you take the shotgun?"

I swallowed, finally admitting my crime. "I came to Maine because the police said my friend Ben had shot himself, but he hadn't. They'd closed the case, run-of-the-mill suicide. I had to find out who really did it. Here, might have been the same thing. His daughter said he was in real trouble, mixed up with some bad people. A suicide probably meant that nobody would dig very hard after that."

She clucked her tongue. "Man, you do have a poor opinion of our investigative skills."

"All from experience."

"Fair enough. Pretty stupid, though to commit a felony and risk going back to prison because of a sense of wanting justice to be served."

"I have poor impulse control."

"I gathered that."

"Did you see where I went to a shrink? He told me I'm pretty messed up and probably have some form of PTSD."

She turned suddenly and glared at me before focusing on the road in front again. My face had damn near melted off from the heat of that look.

I frowned. "What did I say?"

She took a moment before answering. "That's not a term you should use lightly."

I studied her for a few long beats. "Where'd you serve?"

"Over in a sandy place, where we got our asses shot off while a few American companies got rich, if they were connected to the ones that sent us over. I got disgusted and left."

I took a guess. "Army Intelligence?"

Another sharp look, but not as fiery. "You may not be as stupid as you look."

CHAPTER 8

We pulled into the boat landing at the lake and parked. She tossed her suit jacket in the car, and I helped her get the canoe off. As we hoisted it down, her grip slipped and the canoe fell and chunked hard on her left foot. She didn't yell, and there was an odd sound. I looked at her face, and she was frowning and blushing at the same time.

"Service wound. It's plastic now, like a Barbie doll. Couple of extra holes here and there, too. So now you know something about me." She adjusted the pistol in the holster on her belt.

"For what it's worth, I'm sorry. I've got a few wounds, too, but nothing like that."

"Let's get this bitch in the water." Her gruff dismissal told me it wasn't something she enjoyed discussing. But that moment of vulnerability made her more human, and made me feel better about how much she knew about my affairs. She talked tough, sounding like a lot of cops and soldiers and even crooks I'd run into. I knew I sounded like that at times. Some was for show, because she had to put on a rough façade in the alpha-male packs she'd had to run with, but I knew there was some steel in her spine. She could have jacked me up, but was cutting me a break as long as I did her bidding. So okay.

I held the canoe at the shore while she went back to her vehicle. She returned with two paddles, two life vests, and an armload of buoys connected by plastic line. She dumped them in the middle of the canoe. "You're in front."

I had sense enough not to ask if she knew how to maneuver a canoe from the back, and dutifully balanced my way to the front, picking up a paddle. When I was situated, she pushed off and expertly got in without getting her feet wet. No mean trick, so she had some experience.

We paddled in silence, getting the rhythm. I pointed in the general direction of where I'd dumped the shotgun, and she propelled us, following my lead. After a few minutes, I looked around and gauged our position. "Right about here."

She dropped a buoy over the side, and we paddled in a rough circle, dropping the other buoys which were connected by the plastic lines. When we were done, there was an area of the lake surface marked out. I nodded to show I thought it was as good as we'd get.

Without another word, she turned us back the way we'd come, and we paddled back until the bow of the canoe scraped up onto the shore. I jumped out and hauled the canoe up further so she could get out. I held out a hand, but she ignored it and stepped on dry land, perfectly balanced. The artificial foot didn't seem to matter. While she went back to her vehicle to call for the divers, I tied up the canoe and waited.

She came back. "They'll be here soon. I'd told them to be ready for my call. You probably better hide while they're here."

"I appreciate that."

She nodded and wiped her mouth with the back of her hand. "God I could use a cigarette."

I raised an eyebrow.

"No, I quit, but over there, we all smoked. Gave us something to do for the jitters. Filthy habit, but we didn't think it mattered then."

I felt like blurting something out. "I tried to drink myself to death, years ago. My friend brought me to Maine to heal me. That's why I had to check out his murder."

She looked at me with a bemused expression.

I shrugged. "Sorry, don't know where that came from."

"You are one odd duck, I'll grant you that." She almost smiled.

The silence hung there. "So who did Sprague get mixed up with?"

"Don't ask, because I'm not telling you. You really don't want to know. They play for keeps."

I chuckled. "Worse than a Yakuza assassin?"

She grimaced. "Much. The assassin would have killed you quick. Sprague got lucky they didn't want the attention, or they'd have taken their time."

I cocked my head, pondering what I knew of the global criminal world. "Someone from somewhere south of Texas, or east of Vienna?"

She gave me another glass-melting look, and I held up my palms facing her. "Sorry, sorry."

"What part about *'You don't want to know'* didn't you get?"

"Just speculation. Like you, I like to put the pieces together."

"Well don't. This isn't your concern."

"If they're messing about here in Maine, it is."

She looked out over the water. "Let's get the canoe back up. I want to check out the cabin again."

So we hoisted the canoe back up to the top of the vehicle and secured it. I sat while she drove along the road circling the pond to the other side, where my involvement had occurred.

When we'd parked by the little cabin, which had crime scene tape all around, we walked up to the door. I hesitated.

She chuckled. "Crime Scene people have been here, they won't be back. State, not our people. You can leave a trace now, won't matter."

I shrugged. "Could have been awkward, you explaining why you brought me here."

She shook her head. "*Definitely* not completely stupid."

"Uh, thanks?"

"Damn it, they relocked the door. Didn't want anybody wandering in. How'd you get in before?"

"I picked it."

She tilted her head toward the lock. "Work your magic, Mister B and E."

I gave her a sharp look, but took the Swiss Army knife out of my pocket and went to work. I opened it in under a minute, aware of her gaze. I expected a comment, but she said nothing. I stepped back, and she pulled the crime scene tape down and opened the door.

It gave me another chill. The memory of my discovery of the body was fresh. Even with a couple of the shutters open, the interior was still gloomy. She took a small Maglite from her pocket and shone a beam around the place. She stopped on the chair.

"Where was the gun?"

"At the foot of the chair, just to the left."

"Did you touch anything else?"

"No, I stood there for a minute, processing what I was seeing. I carefully picked up the gun, not tracking over the spilled blood, and left."

She snapped the light off. "That was pretty goddamned stupid."

"Not arguing with you. Poor impulse control, like I said."

I couldn't see her face.

"Lot of people in prison have the same problem."

I said nothing. Wisely.

"You could have saved me a barrel of trouble. And we might have found something on the gun that the lake washed off."

"You think they were dumb enough to leave a trace on a careful setup like this?"

She snorted. "No, I'm just pissed at you. I've got to tell a couple of lies on my report about how the assailants ditched the gun on the way out, even though they probably drove here. The fewer lies I tell, though, the better."

"So I owe you one."

"You owe me a lot more than that."

"Find anything on the property? The shed?"

"Nice change of subject," she said. "No, nothing else. They made it look like he just came out with nothing, like he was finding a nice quiet place to blow his head off."

"No ligature marks or injection sites?"

"Playing detective, are we?"

"Just asking."

"Let's get out of here." She led the way back outside, and relocked the door. We stood on the porch for a moment.

"Get one thing straight," she said. "Your part, all your involvement in this is done. Over. You go on your merry way and live your life, while I sort this all out. And try to stay out of trouble from now on, though you being you, I doubt that's possible."

We drove back to the boat landing, and Casey told me to go hide somewhere, as the team would soon be here. I went off into the trees, but stayed close enough to watch. A short time later, an SUV pulled up, with a rowboat on top. Two men got out, and Casey went over and spoke with them. They took down the rowboat and hauled it to the water's edge. They went back into the SUV and brought out a set of scuba gear, and placed that in the boat. Casey handed them a walkie-talkie, while she held another one. The men rowed off.

I could see them out on the lake, at the area Casey had marked. One guy with the scuba gear went overboard. Time passed. The guy came up again, and passed something into the boat. I looked at Casey, who was speaking into the walkie-talkie. She held a thumbs-up.

The men rowed back to the shore, got out, and one handed a shotgun to Casey, who put it into a large plastic bag. She took the walkie-talkie back, then the buoys and rope they had brought back for her, stowing it all in her vehicle's trunk. She spoke to them, and watched as they hoisted the rowboat back onto their vehicle.

After they'd gone, I came out of the woods. She gave me a sour look. "When this is over, you, Mister, are going to buy me a very nice dinner to pay for my time filling out this expenditure report."

"I'd like that," I said.

We drove back to Portland, not speaking much on the way. She dropped me off at my place.

Before I got out, she handed me a card. "That's my cell phone number. Now get out, and try to stay out of trouble. I'd hate to have to cuff you for anything job-related."

I gave her a startled glance, wondering if her words had the playful meaning I thought they did. She was poker-faced, so I wasn't sure.

Dale T. Phillips

A Darkened Room

CHAPTER 9

Miriam had told me that her father's funeral would be the next afternoon in a town called Millinocket, near the Woodville paper company her father had worked for. Woodville was also the town named for the company, just a few miles away, but they were so small they didn't have a funeral home like Millinocket did.

Though I'd been warned to stay away from the investigation, I tended not to take good advice. Anyway it was a public event, and Miriam was going up with a friend of hers and Theo. J.C. and I decided to ride up together, and do a little snooping afterward. He insisted on driving.

We stopped in Bangor for a restroom break and a lunch at DeMillo's, which J.C. said was a long-time establishment. The food was good, and afterward he took me up the road a short distance to the Bangor Fairgrounds, to let me gaze upon the giant statue of Paul Bunyan.

It was impressive, I had to admit. "Thought he was a Minnesota thing."

"That's the subject of heated debate. But Maine is covered with timber country, and he's the quintessential lumberjack. Of course he's ours. People come from all over to look at this statue of a legend and take their picture with him."

J.C. had his press camera and actually did snap a photo of me next to the statue, just like the rest of the tourists. Since he'd paid for lunch, I indulged him. Our viewing done, we got back on the road.

J.C. loved to lecture, and I was a captive audience. "North and east of here, it's pretty much all woods until you get to Aroostook County. Then it's all open farmland for potatoes and beets."

I looked at him. "Hasn't advanced much from the nineteenth century, eh?"

"Part of its charm. There are places here that could be living fifty years or more in the past, as if they were stuck in amber."

"Or some old *Twilight Zone* episode. Just hope we're not going to Willoughby."

He ignored me. "Way back in colonial times, big Maine trees were used for ships' masts.

Lumber has always been central to the region. You know they had a World War Two prisoner of war camp over near Moosehead Lake? The prisoners worked the timber."

"Nothing like good cheap labor who can't complain."

"Thoreau wrote about Moosehead Lake, you know. Biggest mountain lake in the Eastern United States. He loved the place. Remote, beautiful, no people, except for some natives and some lumberjacks.

"Around these parts they used to float the cut logs down the rivers. Guys with axes and peaveys, long poles with hooks, would scamper across the logs to move them around, break up jams. The real Paul Bunyan stuff."

"Sounds romantic, but dangerous as hell."

"You bet. If you fell, you were almost always a goner. Sometimes the jams were so solid, they'd have to use dynamite to break them up. Then back in '71, a paper company built a road almost a hundred miles long, from up in Quebec down to Millinocket. They could then ship by truck, and that was it for the river log drives."

"End of an era. We're near Baxter State Park, aren't we? I've hiked Mt. Katahdin before."

"Yup, to the northwest a little. About 1930, former Maine Governor Percival Baxter bought six thousand acres for a little over four dollars an acre, and he donated the land to the state, which became the park. Over the next thirty years, it grew to about 200,000 acres. It's not even part of the Maine State Park system. They fund it independently through a combination of things."

"So do these towns up here have anything besides the paper companies?"

"Not much. That's why they were built, as a support system. The Woodville company, where Sprague worked, has always been in the shadow of much bigger enterprises that gobbled up everything around. A southern company took over the biggest, Great Northern, a few years back. Woodville's hanging in, but I don't know how much longer they can last."

"You're such a Mainer," I said. "You love this place."

"I do, I love it all. I've been all up and down this state from Fort Kent to Kittery, and from Fryeburg to Passamaquoddy Bay, and everyplace in between. We're the extreme end of the country. There's nothing like it left, except maybe some remote patches in the Pacific Northwest."

I looked around. The only scenery was trees on both sides of the road, almost connecting overhead, like you were going through a forest tunnel. There was no urban clutter, unlike most of the land along Interstate 95, which ran all the way down to Florida along the Eastern Seaboard. Here you could believe you'd gotten away from it all. A big part of why I loved it.

Dale T. Phillips

CHAPTER 10

We arrived at the funeral home early, and there were a few cars already parked outside. J.C. went inside to see if Miriam was there, and how she was doing. Paranoid as I was, I prowled the perimeter of the place, noting exits, the exterior, and the layout of the surrounding buildings. Sprague had been murdered, after all, and Miriam's visitors had meant more trouble. Someone had tried to kill me at an art gallery, after all, so extra caution wasn't such a bad idea.

Inside the building, I looked around where I could, rest rooms, stairwells, closets, and side rooms that weren't locked. A somber-looking bald man in a suit asked if he could help me. I told him I was with Miriam, and he had me follow him.

Miriam was in a large room set up with rows of chairs, her head bent. A woman was with her, probably the friend that had driven her up here. She leaned in to comfort Miriam. Theo and J.C. sat together, a few seats to the right. At the front of the room stood a bier, and a closed casket was on display. No surprise it was closed, considering how I'd found Sprague. To the left was a large photograph of him in better days, to remind people of what he looked like, and to make sure folks knew they were in the right room. To the right was a podium with a microphone.

The smell of the profusion of flowers was overpowering in a ghastly way. Anyone with scent allergies could not have tolerated it.

One other man sat in the back. Since I doubted anyone connected with the funeral home would sit there, I figured he was just one of the mourners who had shown up early. I walked up to him, and gave him a good eyeballing. He must have heard me coming, because he turned to check me out. He adjusted his glasses and looked directly at me, an evaluation. He seemed warier and more alert of his surroundings than most. Interesting.

I addressed him. "Were you a friend?"

"Co-worker," he said. "Norris Deschene. You?"

"Zack Taylor. Friend of his daughter."

"Miriam." He glanced up front. "Seems like she's taking it hard." He looked at me again. "Do I know you?"

"Don't think so."

"I'm good with faces. I've seen you somewhere."

"I don't get up here much."

"It'll come to me."

Once more, I cursed my fifteen minutes of fame while being photographed and written about every time one of the trials came up in which I was involved. The newshounds badgered me and took my photo whenever I appeared near a courthouse, so I got half-recognized a lot like this.

Agent Selkirk came in and frowned when she looked at me. She took off her sunglasses and got right in my face. "What the hell are you doing here? I thought I told you to stay away."

"Nice to see you, too. I'm with Miriam, paying my respects."

She hissed at me a little more, until she noticed Deschene staring at us. She turned her fury on him. "What are *you* looking at?"

He held up his hands, palms out. "Thought you might want to show some respect and take it outside, is all."

She muttered, "I'll take *you* outside, creep," but she broke off and went away.

People began to drift in. Some took chairs, some approached Miriam. The crowd got bigger. Miriam had said there wasn't any after-funeral food-and-condolence thing.

An older man with an oxygen tank on wheels came in and looked around for a seat. I got up and let him have my chair. I saw people looking over at Theo before putting their heads together to whisper. They must not see many large black men in this neck of the woods. He was used to being gawked at, and ignored the stares.

One couple entered after all the seats had been taken. They examined the guest book, the man flipping the pages while the woman had something in her hand and seemed to be taking photos of the signatures, while trying not to look like she was. They didn't sign it. They finished and stood in the back of the room, away from others. People who looked their way gave no sign of recognition.

The couple looked around, carefully scanning the crowd. I made sure I wasn't looking at them when they were looking at me. The man was medium height, trim, and had short-cropped iron-gray hair. He could have been anywhere from thirty-five to fifty-five, but the hard look in his eyes put him on the high end. The woman looked to be late thirties, hair cut soccer-mom short, dressed well, like the man. Running shoes instead of heels. I mentally nicknamed them Ozzie and Harriet, because the man looked a little like Ozzie Nelson from the old TV show.

At the podium in the front of the room, a man was speaking. I tuned out him and the speakers that followed, who said they were from the company where Sprague had worked. A shaky Miriam got up and tried to get through a talk about how she loved her father. Then a woman read a poem, and a song was played over the P.A.

After the orations and service, Miriam stood to the side and greeted people who came up to her to offer condolences and sympathy. There was a long line. Ozzie and Harriet didn't join it. They stood near the exit, looking over every person who left. I contemplated pointing them out to Agent Selkirk.

Someone was speaking in a loud voice. I saw Miriam being confronted by a tall, beefy guy who was wagging a finger in her face. People were pulling back. I moved toward her.

"I'm telling you, he stole from us. And he screwed the sale, which screws all of us. Winslow did us dirt."

"My father would never—"

"Your father lied and took money, and took records. Things are all screwed up now. And another thing—"

He never got to another thing, because Theo grabbed the man's ear and twisted.

"Let's go outside," Theo said, walking toward the door. The ear hold is so painful, you can't do anything but comply. And there are few things more humiliating than being tossed out like that. The offender was protesting rather loudly, but couldn't do much else. I followed.

Outside the building, Theo pushed him away. The man was still whining, and he held his injured ear. He looked like he wanted to fight, or at least say a lot more, but he got a good look at Theo, who stood with crossed arms and a stone-faced expression.

The man turned away, muttering to himself. I went to go back in, and saw Agent Selkirk shaking her head at me. I said nothing as I walked past.

Inside, people were comforting Miriam. She went over and hugged Theo. "Thank you. I don't know why he was saying those terrible things."

"Because he was a drunken idiot. Don't give it another thought."

Theo moved away, and the mourners surrounded her again. I looked around, and Norris Deschene was not in sight.

Ozzie and Harriet were, though, and they looked at each other, and the woman nodded toward the exit. They moved out, and I followed as they walked to the far side of the parking lot, to a large brown sedan.

The guy whirled to face me. "What do you want?"

"Nothing at all. How did you know Winslow?"

"Fuck off."

He got in the car, both of them glaring me like they wished I would melt. I smiled and waved, and focused on their license plate number. When they'd gone, I wrote it on the back of my hand.

J.C. came over and joined me. "What are you doing now?"

"Not much. Following an odd couple. Definitely something funny about them. But if I mention it to the agent in there, she'll just tell me to keep my nose out of it. Maybe they're just weirdos that go to funerals for people they don't know."

"You wrote down their plate number?"

"Yeah. I'm a suspicious bastard. I want to find out more about them."

Dale T. Phillips

CHAPTER 11

We'd come for the funeral, but I wanted to poke around some, despite the warnings from Agent Selkirk. J.C. and I drove over to Woodville. Their main street wasn't much, maybe two dozen buildings. Two banks, a small hardware store, a grocery store, a discount-everything place, a pizza shop, a scattering of office buildings, a gas station at each end of the strip. One bar and grill, a liquor store, and three other bars. So we knew what the local pastime was.

We gassed up at the station on the far side, next to a diner and a little park with a baseball diamond. If you lived here and wanted Chinese food or a dry cleaner, you'd have to go elsewhere. The place wasn't even big enough for any of the chain fast-food joints.

Just past the town was a motel consisting of a main office and eight standalone cabins. Since it looked like our only choice for lodging, we pulled in and parked. The teenager behind the counter looked to be about sixteen, maybe even younger, as she still had braces.

"Hello there, young lady," J.C. used his warm tone, the cheery, avuncular, gregarious one that melted people and made them accept him instantly. I was in awe of his power to make people like him so easily, more so since I usually had the opposite effect. Maybe it was because he truly liked people, and actually understood them. I didn't know if it was because he was a journalist, a student of human nature, or simply that he'd acquired a country wisdom from living in Maine all these years.

"Are you the owner of this business?" J.C. smiled for her.

She blushed and giggled. "No, it's my dad's."

"We'd like one of your cabins, please, one with two beds."

"Sure thing. How long will you be staying?"

"Not sure. We have some business in town, so if it's okay, we'll pay by the day."

"No problem." She quoted a price, and pushed a registration book closer. I laid a pair of twenties on the counter and signed for both of us while she made change. I liked paying cash and remaining anonymous, in case anyone recognized my name from the countless sensational stories that had been published about my adventures. And you could still pay cash in a place like this, no ID needed. So I signed us in as Hank Melville and Nate Hawthorne. No one had ever raised an eyebrow at my literary aliases, and this was no exception.

J.C. was still engaging her in small talk. "If we wanted to get something to eat, where should we go?"

"Probably Bangor," she grinned. "If you wanted something decent, that is. But it's a good forty miles, so if you'd rather stay close, try the Top Hat restaurant, about a half-mile down that way."

"Any particular dishes to avoid?"

"Most of them. The burgers are okay. And the Riverview Diner's alright for breakfast."

"Thank you. We'll take your advice."

She handed us two keys, each attached by a ring to an elongated plastic diamond with the number three stamped on it. We moved the car outside the designated cabin, and took our overnight bags in.

"Well this is cozy," said J.C.

"I've camped in tents that were bigger. With all the available land, they could have added another six feet of room, don't you think?"

"At least it was cheap."

"Still about a dollar a square foot."

"Shall we head out to the aforesaid dining establishment?"

"I can hardly wait."

The Top Hat did not have any Michelin stars for the quality of the food or service. I knew J.C. was hungry, but he didn't finish his burger. I barely got mine down. To add to the insult, their only Scotch was a cheap bar brand, their only beers domestic, and J.C. looked pained at missing out. Well, with any luck, we wouldn't be here long.

In the morning, we had breakfast at the Riverview Diner. A perky young woman served us, and the food was much better than at the Top Hat.

When done, we headed to the Woodville Paper Company, where Sprague had worked. On the way over J.C. casually mentioned. "I called about us doing a feature piece at the company. But we still may not get a friendly reception."

"I'll let you do the talking."

"Always best. Use the camera in my trunk, and we'll say you're my photographer. Take a lot of pictures."

"You have enough film?"

He gave me a look that told me I was the village idiot. "It's digital. No film."

"Oh," I said. "I guess the world is changing."

"Not for you. You should try coming out of your cave once in a while."

"I don't like what I see when I do."

He shook his head, but I didn't know whether in exasperation or agreement. We'd checked a map to get directions to the offices of the paper company. Being the whole reason there was any kind of town here, it wasn't far from the diner. A guard at the gate looked up and set down his magazine. He wore blue jeans, a brown ball cap, and a brown shirt with a patch to show his security status.

J.C. rolled down his window. "We're here to see Howard Merriweather." Merriweather was the Personnel Manager, who also functioned as community relations.

"We're not hiring."

"He should be expecting us."

The man frowned. "Nobody told me."

J.C. waited, smiling. The guard shifted his weight from foot to foot. I guess calling the office was too much trouble, or beyond the guard's imagination. He shrugged and waved his hand in a vague direction. "Office is that way."

J.C. thanked him and we drove through. "Man takes his job seriously." J.C. was grinning.

"Maybe he was cranky because we woke him. Doesn't seem like a lot of action here."

We pulled in to park. J.C. looked at me like a stern uncle would. "Remember, let me do the talking. And try not to hit anybody."

"I find your lack of faith disturbing." I'd heard that line in a movie somewhere.

My reference didn't go unnoticed. "Please don't force-choke anyone, either."

I retrieved the camera from the trunk and took a minute to figure out its operation. We went inside, and asked until we found the right office. Merriweather was a pink, round little man, with a comb-over of a few remaining black strands of hair. He wore a white shirt and a blue tie, and looked over his glasses at us.

"Can I help you gentlemen?"

"I'm, J.C. Reed," said my engaging friend, putting forth his hand. "This is my photographer. I called you about a piece we're writing."

"Oh, sure, sure," Merriweather responded. He barely glanced at me, and didn't offer his hand. He looked at the papers on his desk and drummed his fingers. "I guess I can show you around."

He stood up and came out from behind the desk, all five feet five inches of him. He walked past us and gestured for us to follow him out of the building, talking and gesturing the whole time. J.C. stayed close to him, listening and asking occasional questions, while I took photos and studied the surroundings. I didn't see anything that might yield a clue.

We saw the yards where the big logging trucks brought their loads, and the processing plant. The smell of the chemicals was enough to make you gag. There were massive piles of logs stacked in neat rows, and a few mountains of sawdust. There wasn't much else, and we finished in fifteen minutes. J.C. asked a few more questions, and wrote down some things in a small notebook. I was close enough to hear when he went for the big money line of questioning.

"The papers had a story on an employee of yours that was found dead, possibly murdered. He was an accountant, right?"

Merriweather had been friendly and open, but now his countenance darkened, and he peered over his glasses at J.C. When he spoke, it sounded snappish. "We don't discuss our employees."

"So you don't have any theories on any connections to his death?"

"I hope you're not trying some kind of ruse just to make some sensational story out of a tragedy. I, and by extension, the company, have no comment on that score."

"Certainly," said J.C., apparently unruffled. "It's not what we're writing about, more like professional curiosity, timing and all."

Merriweather finally looked at me. "I'm calling security."

Busted.

CHAPTER 12

The door opened before we could leave. The man who entered was the loner from the funeral, Norris Deschene.

"We meet again," he said, chuckling. "And now I know where I recognized you from, Mr. Taylor. I saw you on TV, on the news a couple of months ago." He looked at J.C., then back at me. "He was there at the service as well."

"You're security?"

"I handle the problems here. And we have one. A big one."

"They were asking about Sprague," piped in Merriweather.

"I'm sure they were. Gentlemen, please come with me."

J.C. and I followed Deschene to his office. He turned to J.C. "I'd like to talk to Mr. Taylor alone."

J.C. waited for my nod, then stepped away.

Deschene sat behind a desk, and I took the chair in front.

"I did some research on you, Mr. Taylor. Asked a few people down state."

"Flattered."

"If you don't mind my saying so, you have somewhat of a sketchy reputation."

"You know how those liars in the tabloids are," I said.

Deschene toyed with a pen. "Winslow Sprague worked here for quite a few years. We thought him a loyal employee, even a friend. But then he up and left, quit us, while taking some valuable papers. Financial records. I'm afraid to say, it may have been to cover some embezzlement on his part."

I said nothing, let him go on.

He looked directly at me. "Funny you should come here like this, because I was going to try to get in touch with you. People say you solve problems. We'd like to hire you to find those records for us. Clear things up."

I yawned. "I'm not a private investigator, nor do I get into business or insurance fraud, if that's what you're after. That's not the kind of work I do."

"You are known in some circles to be rather resourceful."

I shrugged. "The tabloids like to play things up."

"But you do security work, correct?"

"For the right people."

He leaned in. "We've heard Winslow was killed, Mr. Taylor. So there is an element of danger. We don't have anyone with your skills, nor do we wish to put any of our employees at risk. We don't know who we're dealing with, or if those who killed him are after those records."

"But I'm expendable."

He shrugged. "We recognize the risk, and will pay you well. Fifty thousand dollars if you recover our records."

I smiled. My heart was racing, but I kept my outer appearance calm. In poker, if you can, you want to see how high someone will bet in a hand, so you'll know the real stakes. "That's nice money, but it's not worth risking my life, if murderers are involved."

He took a deep breath. "There could be a bonus. He also took well over one hundred thousand dollars from us, along with the records. Anything you find in cash, you can keep. All we want is our stolen records."

"I need to think about it."

He reached into his desk drawer and brought out an envelope and tossed it over. "There's a thousand dollars in there, as a retainer. That should get you started."

I fondled the envelope. I'd thought we were going to get thrown out, but instead I was being offered a job. Of course I was dubious, but why not get paid to do what I was going to do anyway?

Deschene watched me. "So do we have a deal?"

"What's this about, anyway? Why would anyone kill Sprague?"

Deschene tapped the pen on his desk. "I need your assurances that what I tell you does not leave this office."

"Sure."

"We're involved in a major deal to sell the company. There is a lot of money involved, obviously. We don't know why Sprague did what he did, but it means the buyers could back out."

"You had no record backups?"

"He took all of it. The sale is on hold until we recover what he took. It could affect the livelihood of everyone at this company, and this town."

"You know I'm Miriam's friend, but you're telling me her father was a crook."

"The man who accosted Miriam at her father's funeral is Ted Lanella, a VP here. He should not have spoken to her that way. We deeply regret that. But there's a lot of fear. If what Winslow did causes the sale to collapse, the people that live here will suffer. However, if you recover our property, we can forget his thievery."

"Let's circle back to who would want to kill Sprague."

He stopped tapping. "Maybe someone was looking for the money."

"And who else would know he took it? It would be someone in your company, wouldn't it?"

"I doubt it was anybody from here. We're not killers, and we truly need those records back."

"So who, then?"

"Maybe he told someone else. Someone close to him."

"Try another scenario," I said.

He was quiet for a minute. "We had to tell our potential buyers what happened. Perhaps they sent someone to question Sprague who got overzealous."

"Who are these business partners of yours?"

"Abington Associates."

"What do you know about them?"

"They're willing to buy out a troubled concern." He turned his head. "They're listed, legitimate, and can afford to buy our company."

"But maybe these people have some dangerous connections I should be aware of?"

"We don't know. That's why we're offering you a large bonus."

"So I'm a target. Are you going to tell them about me?"

"Of course not. You work for us."

"Maybe."

"You haven't refused the retainer."

Suspicious as I was, I liked getting paid. "Okay then. Deal."

"Here's my card, and my cell phone number. Call anytime."

J.C. frowned at me when I came out. "What did he want?"

"To give me money and send me on a treasure hunt."

CHAPTER 13

Miriam had returned to Portland, saying there was no reason to stay in the area after her father had been buried. Rather than spend another night here, J.C. and I also drove back to Portland, where we had much better dinner options.

I thought about the two men who gained entry to Miriam's house by posing as cops, and Ted Lanella, the VP who had yelled at her at the service. Others might be looking for either the stolen books, or more likely, the stolen cash. So Miriam could be in more trouble than I'd originally thought.

I called Miriam and Theo and offered dinner, my treat. We sat in the upscale place just off Congress, Theo's bulk and dark skin drawing the usual stares.

Theo opened the conversation by tearing out a chunk of my heart. "How's Allison?"

"Why don't you just punch me in the face? She's gone, man. Living with some artist guy in New Mexico, getting famous for her paintings. J.C. says she seems happy. Yay for her. Couldn't take being around me and the violence."

"I miss her."

"*You* miss her? I feel like someone ripped everything from inside me that could feel. I only stayed up here in Maine to be with her. Only woman I've ever loved. Then gone, bam. Out of my life."

Theo was somber. "She thought she was going to get killed."

"I know. I see Ollie coming at me with that shotgun every time I try to go to sleep. If I hadn't had her with me—"

"You might be dead."

I looked away. "Might have been better."

Theo nodded. "Hey, sorry for bringing it up."

Miriam looked at the two of us. "How about changing the subject? Have you found out anything?"

"The man who confronted you at the funeral is a company VP. Deschene and the Woodville staff claim your father departed with a pile of cash and some financial books. So some people are looking for it all, me included. They hired me to find it, and offered a substantial reward."

"Wait," said Theo. "So you're working for Miriam, *and* for the company who claims her father stole from them?"

"If some guy comes along and wants to throw cash my way for doing what I'm already going to do, what am I supposed to do, tell him no?"

Miriam looked a little startled, and I shrugged.

"What if he's setting you up for something?"

"Probably is, but what the hell."

Theo looked thoughtful. "How long do you think she'll need me?"

"Don't know. Two goons posed as cops to get inside her place and question her. I drove them off, but they might be back. Then that jerk accosted her at the funeral home. Somebody might get the idea she knows where the missing money is. She could be in danger. I'm going to go back to Woodville, so I'd like you to continue to keep an eye on her."

Theo nodded. "I heard the cops were grilling you pretty hard."

"They wanted to lock me away. That wasn't the worst of it, though. I've got an FBI agent on my tail."

"What for?"

"They're involved in all this. No idea why. Don't think they do embezzlement— that's more Fielding's area. If he'd been investigating on a Treasury matter, I'd have understood it, since there's money involved. But FBI? Maybe Winslow was into something else, owed money to the mob or something."

"He wasn't like that," Miriam said. "He didn't gamble or chase women, or anything."

I didn't tell her that often people keep surprising secrets, especially from their own flesh and blood.

"Oh, one more thing." I handed Theo a piece of paper with a license plate number. He had some contacts in the Portland Police Department and elsewhere that could check on the registration. I'd got someone in serious trouble for that in the past, but Theo had said it was no big deal. Good thing, as J.C. wouldn't do that for me anymore, and it remained a sore spot between us.

"I'd like to know who this license plate belongs to. Got it from this couple at the funeral home. They didn't seem to be mourning, didn't talk to anyone else, and took pics of the guest book signatures."

I described them, and added the part about Ozzie Nelson. "He practically attacked me in the parking lot when I followed them out. Watch out for them."

Theo sighed. "So you're jumping into a shitpile again." He turned to Miriam. "Sorry."

"Yeah," I said. "It's deep, too. Too many players, too much I don't know. None of this makes sense."

"Please don't do anything dangerous," said Miriam. "I don't want you getting hurt."

I shrugged. *No big loss.*

Dale T. Phillips

CHAPTER 14

The next morning, I drove back to Woodville, where Winslow Sprague had lived in a small house. Miriam hadn't wanted to go with me, as she was emotionally wiped from the funeral, so she'd given me the key to check it out. She told me the police had been out there after Sprague's body was discovered.

Unlike his cabin, it was nice not to have to pick a lock for a change. I opened the door to a mess. Someone else had been there after the police, and before me. Heating grates removed, drawers pulled out and dumped on the floor, pictures ripped from the wall and their backs torn out, contents of cabinets strewn carelessly about. They'd been thorough, and didn't care who knew it. But they hadn't broken the door to get in. So somebody else knew how to pick a lock.

I went through and shook my head at the damage. The TV was still there, as were the liquor bottles, so hadn't been random teenagers on a rampage. This was a deliberate search. Cushions had been ripped open, books pulled from a case and tossed aside in a heap. I went outside and looked around, spotting a number of holes where someone had done quick spade work. Digging for buried treasure?

Someone very much wanted what Sprague had taken. Was it someone else hired by Deschene?

I called Miriam and broke the news. I told her there was little point in calling the police, because whoever had done it would not have left clues as to their identities. I offered to hire a cleaning service in Bangor to come and get the place straightened up, so she wouldn't have to view the mess whenever she decided to come here. She agreed, and I made the call and left instructions and a key where the cleaners could find it.

Back in town, I visited each place of business, trying my darnedest to be the affable curious stranger, channeling J.C. I made a supreme effort to engage people in small talk before mentioning the news story about the guy from here who'd been found dead. Every time I did, the immediate reaction was a frosty chill and the end of conversation. I was beginning to think that the town had a dirty secret that no one wanted to talk about.

Another fruitless afternoon, and an unpleasant reminder of the time that I'd taken on another small town over the question of a woman's innocence. The closed-minded, tribal atmosphere of resentment of outsiders made getting answers impossible. I even dropped by the park, where some kids were playing baseball, and tried to talk to the parents present. I recognized some from the funeral service, but once I mentioned Sprague, they instantly stopped being chummy.

By late afternoon, I was frustrated and grumpy. I went back to the motel to get a cabin for the night. The braces-laden young lady wasn't at the desk, but an older man, thin and, sallow-faced, with a face like a weasel.

"Cabin for the night, please. I just had number three, the Presidential Suite."

Weasel-boy did a double-take. His expression changed as if a skunk had got under the building. "You're that guy who's been all over town, asking about Winslow."

"Yes," I said. "Seems to be a bit of mystery there. I understand he'd lived here for years."

"We don't got any rooms."

"All full up, are you?"

"We don't got any rooms for *you*."

I put my hands on the counter. "Now that's not very friendly." I considered yanking him over the counter by his shirtfront.

He shrank back. "I don't gotta rent to you. You better leave, or I'll call the cops."

In my previous run-ins with small-town police, things had not gone well. The anger swelled up within me, so I decided to leave before I got into more trouble.

I took a drive to calm myself down. I decided to go over to Millinocket and have some dinner, hoping to expand my culinary selections. I found a place that looked half-decent and had a burger. Much better than the Top Hat. When I returned to Woodville, I was in a mellower mood, which would be helpful, as I was going to check out the local bars. Wouldn't do to go in with attitude. I was planning to use my bouncer face from years past, the pose of impassivity. I wondered if I could still pull it off.

A Darkened Room

CHAPTER 15

I went to the first place, sat at the bar, and looked around. Before I even ordered, the bartender said. "You're the fella been asking about Winslow, right?"

"Yeah. Can you tell me anything?"

"No. And you should leave, because no one else will, either. I don't know who the hell you are, but we don't like strangers coming in like you're doing, trying to stir things up."

"I wasn't—"

"Don't care what you was or wasn't. Now get the hell out of my bar."

The second bar I tried had the same result, if just a shade less unfriendly. In the past, I'd shut my emotions down so much that little bothered me, but now I took it as a personal affront when people were rude to my face. My mood was quickly turning to black, a bad sign.

The third bar had deer heads staring into the distance with glassy-eyed indifference displayed on the walls. There were pool tables, but nobody was playing. A few old men drank from long-neck bottles of beer.

I was trying to catch the bartender's attention when three men came through the front door. Two were rough-looking guys who wore boots and had the appearance of men who worked the woods, one with long johns showing under his rolled-up sleeves. The third man was the jerk from the funeral who had yelled at Miriam, Ted something.

Definitely not good.

They held a brief conference and started towards me. I got to my feet, not wanting to get caught sitting in case they jumped me. They set up in the usual way, a triangle with Ted in front, the other two flanking him on either side. Ted eyed me up and down, while the ones in back glared at me. No doubt about it, they were spoiling for a scrap. I was not happy, as I'd been in way too many bar fights.

"Fellas," I said. They seemed the type to rely on their physical size without resorting to other weapons, like knives, but you could never be really sure. I'd have to strike fast if I didn't want to get my ass kicked.

"You were there," said Ted. "The funeral service. You brought that big black bastard, didn't ya? He's not here now, so things are different."

"I suppose so. Say, you wanted to talk about Sprague, but nobody else in town wants to. Why is that?"

He looked taken aback before the sneer returned. "You some kind of cop?"

"Nope. Just hired by Sprague's daughter Miriam to find out about her dad. And you know things about him. Want to tell me?"

"He was part of this town, one of us. But when a deal came that would help us, he messed it up. Took some records and some money, left us in the lurch."

"That what everyone thinks? That he took the money and ran? Left behind a house and a place he'd called home for years? Just to go to Portland?"

"That's what happened."

"Doesn't make much sense, does it? Maybe there's something more."

Ted wasn't about to give it up. He'd been humiliated, and would want to get some of his pride back. So he'd push.

"You calling me a liar?"

"No, there's just more to the story. So why are you getting mad at Miriam and me?"

He ignored the question. "Where's the other one that was with you? The old guy?"

"He left before the trouble started."

"What trouble?"

"The kind there'll be if you lay your hands on me."

He grinned. "No need of that, if you leave now. We'll escort you."

I didn't believe him as far as I could throw this bar. He just wanted to get me outside, where they wouldn't mess the joint up. "Nah, I'm staying right here, in front of witnesses."

Ted nodded. "Okay, then." He half-turned away, and the punch was so telegraphed, it might as well have been Western Union. I knocked his arm to the side, slipped past him, and aimed a kick at the kneecap of the guy to his left. The blow hit solid, he yelped, and then number three was on me, swinging away. I blocked some heavy hits and snapped a finger thrust to his throat before the first guy bear-hugged me and drove me back into the bar. I head-butted his face while stomping on his instep, and his arms loosened just enough for me to break his grip. I drove a palm up under his chin, and barely blocked a wild punch coming in from my left. We were a tangle of arms and legs, and some of the shots were getting through, including one on my ear that hurt like hell, and made a ringing sound. I'd been right about them being tough. They were scrappers for sure. I wasn't sure I'd come out of this in one piece.

A woman's voice cut through our action loud and clear, and imperious as hell. "FBI! Nobody move."

We all froze in place. Cautiously, I snuck a glance, and saw Agent Selkirk standing there, eyeballing the three fighters like she was daring them to recommence their pounding of me. She hadn't even drawn her weapon yet. They backed away, and I didn't care if they were cowed, or just startled enough to let up.

Selkirk pointed at me. "*You*. Come with me."

And I did, happy enough to escape the rest of the fight.

Dale T. Phillips

CHAPTER 16

Outside of the bar, she whirled to face me. God, she looked fierce. "What in the HELL do you think you're doing?"

"Asking questions. Were you following me?"

"No, I was doing my job, and got word of some nosy clown going around asking about Sprague. I should have let you get your ass kicked."

"That's harsh."

"You don't know from harsh yet. So now you're playing detective, huh? Want an obstruction of justice charge?"

"I just wanted to see if someone knew anything about why Sprague ran, and who might want to kill him."

"Hey, dumbass, that's what *I'm* here for. YOU don't have a badge, so YOU cut the shit.

I don't want you anywhere near this case. Or your buddies, either. Where are they?"

"Back in Portland."

"Then they've got more sense than you. Why were you doing this, anyway?"

"Sprague's daughter Miriam hired me to find him and protect him. I didn't, so I feel I owe her at least an explanation for how and why he died. And she's in more trouble. When I went to her place, before the funeral, two goons with guns were there, posing as police."

"You didn't tell me that. I said to tell me everything."

I spread my hands. "Sorry. Slipped my mind when you were threatening me."

"Might follow through on that. Give me all the details."

I looked around. "Well, I need to find a place to stay. The owner of the one motel in town told me I was no longer welcome at his establishment."

"You do have a talent. Fine. You can stay with me. I need to keep an eye on you anyway, to make sure you don't get into any more trouble. But don't get any ideas. There's two beds in the room, so be grateful you're not sleeping on the floor."

I wisely kept my mouth zipped shut.

I got to my car and followed her back to the motel. When I got out, weasel-boy came out of his office, saw me, and yelled. "I told you to get out. You ain't staying here."

Selkirk flashed her badge. "I am an FBI agent, and this man is a material witness under my protection. Go back inside, sir."

He looked like he was going to protest further, but she cut him off. "This is a federal matter, end of discussion. Understand?"

He looked like he wanted to argue, but he got smart. He muttered something under his breath and went back inside, slamming the door.

Selkirk got an overnight bag and another one from the car and went to her unit. She set down her bags, and took out her service revolver. She held it in one hand while she unlocked the unit with a key, keeping to the side rather than right in front of the door. She snaked a hand in and flicked the light on, and pushed the door open. She crouched and poked her head around the jamb. She stood and motioned me to enter. When we were inside, she holstered her gun, bolted the door, and wedged a chair under the lock. Anybody trying to kick the door in would have a lot more resistance than they bargained for.

"I thought *I* was paranoid," I said.

"If you knew what you'd gotten yourself into, you'd be a lot *more* paranoid."

"I'll bite. What did I get myself into?"

"Deep shit. You get the far bed."

She sat in the remaining chair, took out a laptop computer, and flipped the lid up, and went to work.

"Okay. Tell me about the two fake policemen."

I gave her a full report, with descriptions as best as I could. She typed away as I spoke, asking questions until she'd gotten everything.

"If that's it, I'm going for a run. I won't be able to sleep, and don't want to keep you up."

"No. You're staying here."

"You can drive alongside if you want, but I'm going. I know it's a risk, but it's mine to take."

"Why don't you ever do what you're told?"

"Force of habit. Look, I've got a mobile phone. I'll call if there's any trouble, and you can come save me again."

She opened her mouth to say something more, then her gaze softened. She sighed. "I used to run. Miss it."

"You could come with me."

She shook her head. "I've got work to do."

I ducked into the bathroom to change. She was still pounding away on her machine when I moved the chair, unlocked the door, and slipped out into the darkness.

There were no streetlights out here in the middle of nowhere, but the moon was out, giving an ethereal glow to the road. I set an easy pace, jogging along as I let my mind go empty. There was no traffic either, and the night sounds were peepers and various nocturnal creatures. I saw a bat swooping near a tree, swallowing mosquitos, and heard an owl hoot. The woods always rejuvenated me, and the knots in my mind began to unravel a bit.

Sweat popped out all over me, and thoughts dissolved into a physical reverie, breathing in and out, feet rising and falling along the blacktop. Despite my troubles, I'd found a measure of peace in Maine, so different from the life I'd led in cities like Miami and Las Vegas, with their ever-present lights and ever-present sirens, and people and urban noise. Most of the small population of this state lived in the cities and towns to the south and southwest of here, many along a narrow strip along each side of Interstate 95. There were huge swaths of land, thousands of acres of woods. To the north and west was the Allagash, a massive expanse of wilderness swamp and waterways, a land of blood-sucking insects, moose and bear, and little else. Baxter State

Park was nearby, with the majestic, mystic, mile-high Mount Katahdin rising from the land in a solitary monument; much like Ayers Rock does in Australia. To the north was Aroostook County, another vast landscape, of rolling hills that had been formed by the scouring of glaciers long before. There wasn't a great deal east of here until you hit Canada. So much pristine wilderness, still undeveloped in this day and age. I'd lived in a number of places, but had adopted Maine as my home.

By the time I got back to the motel, I was pleasantly exhausted, all my nervous energy burned away, along with the negative thoughts. I took off my sweat-soaked T-shirt and wiped my face. I knocked and waited for Selkirk to let me in. I announced myself and she cracked the door to check before letting me through the door, then holstering her service revolver, which she'd had ready. Good precautions.

As I made a beeline to the bathroom to shower, I noticed her staring at me. "What?"

Her look was solemn. "You've been banged up a little, that's all."

I wasn't normally self-conscious about the many scars that dotted my hide, but now I felt naked. I knew my battered body looked like someone had repeatedly dragged me through broken glass mixed with barbed wire, and the faded, reddish punctures and crooked seams ran like a relief map all over me.

"It's okay," she said. "I've got a bunch of scars myself."

I went into the bathroom and showered, now aware that I was in a motel with a desirable woman, albeit one who held my fate in her hands. I tried not to think of how attracted I was becoming as I changed into a clean pair of shorts and a T-shirt.

When I got out, she was in bed, tapping on her laptop. She sipped from a cup of something, and I smelled liquor. She didn't offer me any, for which I was grateful.

She looked up. "Hope you didn't want to watch TV."

"I usually read at night, but I don't have a book. The run tired me out, so I might be able to sleep now."

She spoke something barely audible. It might have been "Lucky."

Dale T. Phillips

CHAPTER 17

My run hadn't tired me out enough for my brain to shut down, so of course I lay awake, thinking and going over the day. I shut off my bedside light, but it was a while before Selkirk finally closed her laptop. The room was still and dark. I could hear her breathing and knew she remained awake as well. It was some time before I finally dropped off, wondering which ghosts from my past would come visit this night.

A hoarse cry wrenched me from sleep, and I was up out of the sheets and ready to tackle whatever menace had arrived. I snapped on the light. Selkirk was sitting up in bed, wide-eyed and looking confused, her breathing ragged. I went to her.

"It's okay," I said. "Just a bad dream."

She looked at me for a moment like she didn't recognize me. She blinked, shook her head, and sobbed. I put my arms around her.

I spoke quietly, and we rocked back and forth. "It's okay, all over. All over. You're safe now." I continued murmuring reassuring words.

She gently pushed me away and wiped her eyes. I handed her a tissue, and she blew her nose in it. "Sorry."

"For what?" I went back to my bed. "I do the same, at least twice a week."

"So much blood," she said. "I was back overseas, when we got blown up." She rubbed her face. "My ears were popping, there were guts and brain matter everywhere, I couldn't see anything else, just a red mist, and my foot was shredded into a pulp. I couldn't feel it yet, couldn't feel a thing. Jesus."

"I don't know how anyone gets over that kind of thing," I said.

"This helps," she said, reaching over the side of her bed to bring up a bottle. She poured a goodly slug into the cup on the stand by her bed. "Want some?"

"No thanks."

She drank deeply, poured some more, capped the bottle, and set it back. She lay back against the wall and sipped her drink.

She sighed. "Worst of it is, we had no reason to be there. None. The British got their asses kicked when they were the best military power in the world. The mighty Russians got knocked to shit, and then we strolled in like we're any better, and just hung around getting shot at. With the weapons we'd given them to fight the Russians. Waste of billions of taxpayer dollars. Stuck our eagle beak in, for no earthly reason, and now we were the enemy, just like Russia had been."

She fingered the glass, her mind halfway across the world. "And I got this souvenir courtesy of those bastard Russians." She poked the sheet up a few inches with her plastic foot. "Fucker mujahedeen on a rooftop with a leftover Russky RPG. Blew chunks out of us, and bye-bye, little piggies, and high heels. That was it for me."

She drank some more. "Got out on disability, came back stateside, but couldn't sit around after that, needed some action. Civilian life was too boring. I was drinking too much. Applied to the FBI. A few adjustments had to be made, but an ex-military senator with some juice dropped not-subtle hints to the FBI brass there that I'd better pass, no matter what it took, because I was owed. After what I'd been through, training at Quantico was a breeze, and my foot didn't slow me down much, once I'd got used to it. I suppose the training would be tough if you've never done anything like it. I mean, some washed out. But when you shoot at targets, they don't shoot back."

She snorted. "But shit, they should call it the Federal Bureaucracy of Investigation. Everything by the goddamn book. Image over effectiveness, too."

I had no idea what to say. I'd never served, never thought about going into the military. Or law enforcement.

She set her glass on the stand. "Turn the light off."

I did, and she got up and stumbled a bit on her way to the bathroom. I pretended to be asleep when she came back, though I knew she wasn't fooled. We both lay in the dark, in our own private hells of remembering, and it was a long time before I got back to sleep.

CHAPTER 18

Morning light struck my eyes. I opened one.

Selkirk came out of the bathroom and made a sweeping motion with her arm. "All yours."

I'd slept for maybe four hours, and right through her rising and showering. I showered and dressed. When I came out, she was pecking away at her laptop, alternating with writing something in a notebook and flipping pages. Her hair was pulled back in a bun. Looked pretty good for the few hours of sleep she'd got. There was no mention of last night, and I wasn't going to bring it up.

She looked up. "Breakfast and coffee. You in?"

"Hell, yes," I said.

She locked her laptop in the car trunk. We drove to the diner and sat at a booth. We scrutinized the big plastic menus, and a waitress came up to the table.

"Hey, how's it going? Welcome back." This was to me.

"Hi Beth." She'd served J.C. and me at our last meal here, and I'd remembered her name from her nametag.

"Coffee?"

We both agreed.

Beth walked away, and Selkirk looked at me before shaking her head.

"What?" I couldn't tell what she was thinking.

"Beth." She nodded in the direction of the departed.

"What about her?"

"She's got a crush on you."

"What? She's just a child."

"If twenty is child age, then yeah. But she lit up like a Christmas tree when she saw you. Didn't like seeing me, though. She's got it bad for you."

"Oh, please."

"You really have no idea, do you?"

"Change of subject. What are you having?"

"The entire left side of the menu."

I grinned. Beth came back with our coffees, then went back for the juice and water. She took out her pad. "Know what you're going to have?"

As Selkirk ordered, I watched Beth's face. When she walked away, Selkirk raised her eyebrows.

"You called it," I said. "I didn't have a clue. I never did anything to encourage her."

"You didn't have to. Just be yourself. So. A youngster with braces and daddy issues."

"You're not as funny as you think you are."

Her eyes twinkled. "Oh, come on. I'm going to have some sport with this, keeping you from the clutches of small-town women."

"Ordinarily, I'd like your sense of humor." I put sugar in my cup, and added the contents of a creamer.

"Can't take it?"

"Not before coffee."

"Well drink up, then," she said cheerily. "It's going to be a long day."

Our food arrived, and we tucked in. She ate like she hadn't seen a meal in a week, and I did the same. I liked a big breakfast to fuel up for the day, and it seemed like her style as well. We finished and sat back with contented sighs.

"Wish I still smoked," she said. "I'd love one right about now."

"So now what?"

"Think I'd better keep an eye on you, to make sure you don't get into any more shit. You're a one-man wrecking crew. You don't just meet trouble halfway, you hunt it down and drag it from its lair."

"Is your office going to accept you babysitting me?"

"Let me worry about that. My case, my rules. You're a material witness, and I have to keep you safe."

"I've been pretty good at keeping myself safe up until now."

She laughed. "Oh, yeah, real safe, with those railroad tracks of scars all over your body. You look like you've been used for a human piñata."

"I was. But I'm still here."

She gave me a piercing look. "Ollie Southern almost got you. Twice."

"Same answer."

"You realize it's all a matter of luck, right? And someday your luck is going to run out."

I knew she was right, but didn't want to admit it.

We paid the tab, and left a good tip. Beth scurried over to give me an effusive goodbye, and I studiously avoided looking at Agent Selkirk.

We went to her car and buckled up.

"Where are we going?"

"Back to the mill. I've got some more questions for those people."

We were already headed out of town. I frowned. "Aren't you going to drop me off by my car first?"

She took her eyes off the road for a moment to give me some side-eye. "Actually, I should cuff you to the wheel and let you stew for a bit. Let you know the penalty for screwing around with my investigation."

"You still haven't told me what you're even investigating."

"The less you know, the better."

"Most of the time when I'm really curious, I go looking for answers on my own."

She gave me the look again. "I really should have you locked up until this is over."

I decided to shut up. We were coming to a small bridge over a stream, with a steep drop-off on my side, and she slowed. We crossed over, and from our left a pickup truck came roaring at us, smashing into her driver-side door. Our car cracked through the guardrail and plummeted in a sideways roll down the embankment.

The car smacked hard and stopped rolling. We were upside down, but still alive. The vehicle swayed in an uncertain rocking motion.

I swallowed a couple of times and got my wind back, adrenaline surging through my system. "You okay?"

"Sorta," she gasped. "Don't move. Don't even fucking breathe."

"What is it?"

Her voice was high, strained. "We hit something that stopped us, maybe a rock, but I'm looking down below me at what's got to be at least a sixty-foot drop, with nothing else between us and the bottom. No way we'd survive that. If we slip off whatever we hit, we're falling onto those rocks. And we don't seem very stable."

"Jesus. What do we do? Stay here until help comes?" I looked out my cracked window at the top of the slope, about thirty feet up.

"I can't reach my phone. No telling how long until someone comes out this way, especially with the right equipment. We're fucked."

I attempted to swallow again, but couldn't quite manage it. I tried to control my rising panic. "So we can't stay here, and we can't move. About sum it up?"

"You might be able to roll out," she said. She sounded a lot calmer than I felt. One damn cool customer, talking about her own demise.

"Let's both get out. Real slow, real careful."

I braced myself and unbuckled, shifting a little as gravity took hold. The car gave a menacing sway, and I yelped and stopped moving. "Damn."

Her voice was quiet, but resolute. "You make sure they get the fuckers that did this, or I'll come back from the grave and haunt you. And have my people retrieve my laptop from the trunk."

My mind was spinning, weighing options. "I've got a plan. If you can unbuckle and scootch a little sideways, you can point up. I'll open the door and ease out just a little, look for a handhold on the bank. You hold my legs. If the car falls away, we can maybe push out and shoot through the opening, not go with it."

"Too risky. No sense taking you down, too."

"No time for heroics. Do it. Get yourself unbuckled."

"Try opening the door first. If it goes, get yourself out."

I couldn't argue with her any more. I slowly moved the handle to click the passenger-side door latch loose. Then I eased it up and away from the car body. I had to twist and shift my weight to get leverage, and the car shuddered with heart-stopping motion. But we stayed put, and I pushed the door out enough that it held, pointing straight up.

"Okay, now you," I said.

I couldn't see her, but I heard the click, and felt the car lurch as she slowly squirmed around to face up in the same direction I was.

"You good?" I could hear the two of us breathing very loudly.

"I think so."

"Okay, I'm going to find a handhold. Get ready to grab my legs."

The roof of the car was against the ground, and I felt around outside until I got hold of a root of some kind. I pulled on it, increased the pressure, and it only gave a little. It would have to do, as it sounded as if the car was sliding off its precarious perch and succumbing to gravity.

I pulled on the root with both hands as if I was chinning myself, and was halfway out of the car. Selkirk gripped my leg.

"If you're clear, push up," I said. "If it goes, thrust hard."

Hearing a horrid screech of metal tearing away from rock, I pushed up and away with my free leg, and the car fell away around me. She came out of the car like being birthed, then her weight pulled on my leg. The vehicle no longer encased us, and the smash from below told me the rest.

It wasn't a straight ninety degrees up, but it was steep, and there wasn't a lot to grab. My dead friend Ben and I had done a little rock climbing, but it had been years ago. "Dig your feet in," I gasped. With the weight of two of us on it, some of the root pulled out from the bank. I kicked my free foot into the earth to gain an extra hold. Below me, I could feel Selkirk doing something similar.

"You secure?" At least some of the weight was off.

"Yeah."

"Okay, move one hand until you get a secure handhold. "

"Got it."

"Test your weight before doing the other hand. Slow and easy."

She released my leg. "Okay, I'm good. I've done this before, you know. Just never while hanging off someone."

I was beginning to think we might get to live a little longer. I was cautiously feeling around for secure holds when Selkirk came alongside me and kept going higher.

She flashed me a dazzling smile as she passed, as if she was now enjoying herself.

"Race you to the top."

Dale T. Phillips

CHAPTER 19

Selkirk and I climbed up to the road, much the worse for wear, but alive. We flagged down a passing car, made a call from a phone, and she started the wheels of justice. After a brief statement, local law enforcement put out a notice for the black pickup that had almost killed us, but that kind of vehicle was depressingly common in these parts. We spoke at length to the cops, and promised to return the next day, but told them we hadn't seen anyone driving, just that big-ass grill coming at us faster than she could react.

Her federal status helped cut a lot of red tape. FBI agents would get a retrieval team for the car, and recover the laptop.

We were cleaned and patched up at the hospital in Bangor, while we gave statements to the state police. Nothing broken, no concussions, just banged up pretty bad. One of her people went out and got us some new clothes, fresh but stiff, hastily purchased in approximate sizes at the nearby mall. Her purse was still in the car, so the agent also gave her a credit card to use for the time being.

It was dark before we were alone together. We picked up some takeout from a Chinese food place, and rented a hotel room near the airport. We were exhausted, neither of us wanting to do anything but recuperate.

We ate our food in the room and sat with our thoughts. Casey took out a brown plastic vial of pills and shook a few into her hand, swallowing them down. She took a bottle of tequila from a brown paper bag.

"That a good idea?" I showed my disapproval. "Booze and pills together?"

"Piss off," she said. "I'm hurting. Done this before, you know. After my foot, I got to love morphine for a time, and I'd drink along with it. Finally had to kick the stuff. But man, while it was taking the pain away, I understand why they called it Soldier's Joy. That's a Civil War song."

"I know."

She unwrapped the top and unscrewed the bottle. She drank.

"Look, I know we had a close shave and all—"

"We didn't have a *close shave*. We almost fucking *died*. This close." She held her forefinger and thumb together, not apart.

My aching body remembered.

"And you know the worst of it? I fucking love it. I'm higher than a kite. I haven't felt an adrenaline jolt like that since I came back from overseas. You saved us. Pulled us out of a deathtrap."

She was talking fast. "You hear about adrenaline junkies, the rush and all, but until you feel it, you don't get it. Once you've been there, regular life is boring and gray."

"I know," I said. In my brushes with death, I'd also felt the unworldly exhilaration that comes from having escaped the clutches of the Reaper. It made me feel superhuman, like I could do anything. Maybe that's why I so often took stupid chances.

"Yeah, you get it. You've been there. So you know there's no goddamn way I can get to sleep tonight without help. Because once these jitters wear off, then it's back to the trauma." She looked back at the bottle. "I need this. It turns off the switch. After sundown, the dead come out, whisper in my ear. I can see their faces, too."

"It's the same for me," I said, my mouth dry. "My horror is black snakes squirming around inside, gnawing at me."

She nodded. "So join me." She waved the bottle. "Drown those fuckers."

"It'll kill me. I don't have the off switch. If I start again, I'll never stop."

She looked at the bottle like a shipwrecked person views a rescue boat. She licked her lips. "Well, I'm still going to."

I took the plunge. "Well, I was hoping to kiss you, but if you drink more, I can't. I wouldn't know which taste I was falling for."

She stopped and stared at me. "Best be real careful what you say next, partner. You're about to go over another cliff."

"Look, I'm really attracted to you. It's not just what we went through together. You've been to the darkness, so you know the places I come from. But drinking just makes things worse. I have to focus on something else, something outside of myself. It's the only thing to push the pain away. That's why J.C. brings me all the strays. I'm Portland's patron saint of lost causes, the court of last resort for the desperate and hopeless. If I live one more day, maybe I can do some good. But if I fall, they fall."

She nodded. "That's why I'm so damn good at my job. I drive my ass to exhaustion, but most of the time even that doesn't work. So I unplug the jug. My foot wasn't the first blown-off body part I saw over there. That's why I still can't ever eat hamburger."

"Let's try another way to forget. Come to shore instead of drowning."

She stood up, and I embraced her. We clung to each other. She let go and took hold of the bottle. "Can you make me forget for a while? Can you take my mind away as good as this can?"

"That's a dead-end path. Why don't we celebrate life, instead?"

She put the bottle back in the bag with a wistful look. "What the hell? Let's try it."

We tried it. We celebrated life, and each other. We were glad as hell to be alive. I didn't know about her, but I certainly forgot my problems in our frenzied coupling.

I slept like the dead, and didn't see the ghosts that night.

Dale T. Phillips

CHAPTER 20

A sharp cry of pain snapped me awake. I tried to get up, but my body felt as if I'd gone fifteen rounds of a kickboxing match against a tough opponent. I gasped and did a mental systems check as a shaft of morning sun peeped through the gap in the hotel curtains. Memory flooded in, and I turned a stiff neck to see Casey lying next to me, swearing softly.

"You okay?"

"No," she responded. "Did we get in an accident or something?"

I chuckled. "Two, I'd say."

"Yeah. Second was definitely much better. But ow. Jesus, I think I pulled something."

"Me too."

She groaned. "Can you move?"

I tested. "A little."

"Good. Get up and get my pills from the dresser over there. And some water."

I eased myself upright, aware I was naked. I shuffled across the room, hearing a snicker from the bed.

"Who are you, old man? Last night I was being ravaged by some vigorous young guy."

I huffed. "I'm getting too old for car accidents and crawling up cliffs."

"What about sessions of hot monkey love?"

"If we can do the second part without the first."

"I've never been this sore after sex. Hurry up with those pills."

I read the printed instructions on the vial. "Says you're not supposed to take them on an empty stomach."

She swore again. "Any leftovers from last night?"

"Couple of fortune cookies."

"Good enough."

Palming the pill bottle, I swept up the two wrapped cookies and moved to the bathroom. I ran some water in a cup and brought it all back to her. She'd pulled the sheet up to her neck. Her sudden modesty surprised me after the abandon of the night before, but then I remembered that she was self-conscious about her scars.

I moved closer, and stubbed my toe on something. It was her service weapon, right next to the bed. Even in all our frenzied disrobing, she had presence of mind to keep her gun by her side. I looked over to the door, and as I expected, she had wedged a chair under the lock. Total pro.

As I stood next to the bed with my hands full, she reached out and took hold of my penis, bobbing it up and down like she was shaking hands.

"Hello, new friend," she giggled. "Pleased to make your acquaintance."

"Let go," I said. "That's the only part of me not sore."

"We could fix that, maybe in about a week, when I recover. Now give."

She uncapped the pill bottle and shook out four of the little white lozenges. She tossed them in her mouth and I handed her the water. She swallowed, and I traded her the cookies for the cup.

She shook the pill bottle. "Want some?"

"Yes," I said, taking two. She handed one of the cookies back. I set down the water and unwrapped the cookie. I crunched the sweetness and looked at the fortune inside.

"You will make a new friend," I said.

"*In bed*," she finished. "Well, that one was on the money. Mine says 'Be careful of new ventures. *In bed*.' Man, whoever was writing these had our number."

"You want the shower first?"

"No," she said. "I'm going to lie here and wait for the pills to kick in. You go ahead. Just don't use up all the hot water."

The hot spray felt great as I gradually steamed some of the ache from my body. By the time I finished, the painkillers were taking effect, and I was halfway to human. In the bathroom mirror, I noticed that along with a few facial cuts, I had a beauty of a black eye. I had a host of cuts, scrapes, and bruises, but our checkup had shown nothing broken or more serious. I applied fresh dressings from the extras we'd been given, then emerged and put on the same ill-fitting clothes that had been bought for me, as she watched me from the bed.

I found my wallet and tucked it in my pants. "You okay with me going out for coffee while you get ready? Didn't want you to think I was ditching you."

"If you bring me back decent coffee, I'll put you in my will. Two creams, four sugars."

I made my way out, and went in search of caffeine. Next to the coffee shop was a drugstore, so I went in and bought a few items. I walked over to get two large coffees and went back to the room.

She answered my knock. "Who is it?"

"Coffee delivery."

There was some clunking as she removed the chair she'd replaced after I left. She really did take precautions.

She opened the door. "Get in here."

I stepped in and handed her one of the large foam cups. She flipped the top off and drank.

"Ow."

"It's hot," I said.

"Yeah, no shit. I don't care. Oh God, that's good."

She wore her new clothes, her hair pulled back. She looked refreshed, but yesterday's crash had marked her up as well. She had a nasty cut on her lip, a bruise, and like me, a bit of a shiner. Her nails were ruined from our cliff climb.

I opened the drugstore bag and took out the items. "Toothbrushes and toothpaste. Sunglasses for our raccoon eyes."

"You couldn't get me some makeup? I can't walk around with my face like this. They'll think you did it."

"Uh, sorry," I said. "I wouldn't know what to get."

She laughed. "I'm just messing with you. Of course you wouldn't know. But our first stop is a makeup section. I look like a witch."

"You look great."

"Have a seat. We need to talk."

Four of the scariest words one can hear. I sat, and she sat on the bed. She blew on her coffee and drank some more, then set the cup on the stand by the bed.

"I feel like a shit for doing this after what we've been through, but we've got to get some things straight."

I waited, silent.

"Last night was great. More than great. You saved my life, we cheated death, we needed it. I used you. Don't think you minded much, but this isn't going to continue. I'm on the case, and nothing is going to get in my way, especially now. I've called in the cavalry, and we're going after these fuckers with all guns a-blazing. When they feel bold enough to try to kill an FBI agent, it's time to run up the black flag and burn them to the waterline.

"If you hadn't been with me, I'd have died, and I'm grateful. But also guilty. We don't involve civilians. So I need you to fade back and keep your nose out of this. And I can't be distracted. God knows, you distract the hell out of me. But I'm on the warpath, and that's all my focus. Got it?"

I nodded, having noticed she was talking more like a hard-ass soldier. "Okay, I get it. All professional from here. But I need to know what we're up against."

"There's no we."

"When someone tries to kill me, I at least need to know who they are and why."

She looked at me for a long moment. "Fine. Take me to breakfast, and I'll tell you why you're in deep shit."

Dale T. Phillips

CHAPTER 21

Before we got breakfast, Casey made us go back to the drugstore, where she picked up a few items of makeup. She spent some time in the car, using the visor mirror to apply a few things. When she was finished, with the big sunglasses on, you couldn't tell she'd been smashed up and driven over a cliff.

We found a diner, got a corner table away from other people, and both ordered huge meals. She'd popped more painkillers and had more coffee, so she was perky and talkative. About everything else but what I wanted to hear.

I interrupted. "Look, I know you don't want to tell me, it's an ongoing case and all. But who the hell are bold enough to go after the FBI?"

She swirled a spoon around in her coffee. "Russians."

"What? You're kidding."

"I wish I was. When the Soviet Union fell apart, Russia was still in the game. Some people there are spreading their tentacles again, seeing where they can influence things. But this time it's not political, it's money. The new god.

"When certain factions in a country have sucked their own neighborhoods dry, they have to go elsewhere for new opportunities. They look for easy pickings, places where there's not a lot of competition. Chunks of territory to control, on a world-wide scale. Billions at stake."

I drank my own coffee and thought about this. "A giant game of RISK, combined with Monopoly."

"Yup. So of course there's competition. When it happens, you can go head-to-head, or you can go sly and try a lot of back channels. So there's a thousand tiny battlegrounds, for little pieces of the pie. Butterfly effect. Put a little pressure here, cause a disruption there."

"Don't tell me Maine's one of those battlegrounds."

"It is. They're going after the lumber company that Sprague worked for."

A Darkened Room

"But why? Russia's got plenty of forests. They don't need Maine lumber."

"But Japan does."

I looked at her. "Russia and Japan in a trade war? Didn't they have a real war, about a century ago?"

"This one's all about the money."

Our waitress brought our food, and we dug in, pausing between bites.

I couldn't figure it. "So how does taking over a Maine lumber company hurt the Japanese?"

"One supply source cut off. Then another, and another. When the Russians have got the lumber all locked up, no more wood from the northeast. Multiply that times the other places they do it, and one day there's a real shortage back in Japan, resources harder to get. You either pay a lot more, work a deal while giving up major concessions, or go without. Soon it looks like their government doesn't get global trade. Shortages like that mean public scrutiny of government policies, and sometimes changes in government. Loss of confidence, even maybe a new election, with people more favorable to outside interests. Or just the threat of it, for leverage for better terms on some agreements."

"Wow."

"You saw some of that with Harada. There's more interest in North Atlantic fishing than you realize, more than sea urchins, and not just Maine. Japan's appetite is voracious, and they're competing to get all they can before the stocks totally collapse. Did you know that the cod off our shores were once so thick, you could almost walk across the water on them at some points? Now we've stripped the oceans dry, wiped out whole species of fish. It's just a question of time before they're all gone. So the Russians are moving in on the companies that sell to Japan. You of all people should notice the Japanese boats are no longer around Portland."

"Yeah, I thought they left because Harada was killed."

"In a sense, they did. His island was bought by a corporation that has so many shell companies, it's like those Russian dolls. *Matroishka*, I think they're called. But I'll bet you a year's salary if you get to the last one, it's got those Russian backwards p's. Same group going after Sprague's company. So many subsidiaries and shells to get through, but the heart is red."

"So the Russians are going after lumber and fish. What else?

She waved a fork. "Cars. The US is a major market for Japanese cars. Say there's one dealership that sells Japanese cars. Then a few other dealerships move in around it to sell Swedish, German, even American cars, at bargain prices. Nothing major by itself, but each taking a piece of business away, chipping away at the margins, until it's no longer profitable to sell those Japanese models in that location. Buyers have to go farther out, maybe decide to try something closer to home. Dealerships change hands or change what they sell. And it's happening across the country."

I put down my fork. "So they've got the world mapped out like a giant go board, with hundreds of pressure points. The Russians stake a position, like placing a stone on the board. By itself, it's nothing. The Japanese ignore it, or respond to it. Some points get hard fought, some are ceded without a struggle. But without opposition, soon there's a string of stones, a solid base."

She grabbed a forkful of hash browns off my plate.

I mused. "How'd you find out about all this?"

She sighed. "In Afghanistan, as Army Intel, we turned up a lot of weird shit, some of which you would just not believe. After the Russians left, there wasn't a lot of love for them. I ran across one old guy who spun me a tale about a war between the bear and the rising sun. Just like 1905, like you said. Maybe the Russians are still pissed about losing that one. I didn't believe it at first, and there wasn't much I could do about it anyway. We had other priorities, like staying alive.

"When I got back, I joined the Bureau. Most of our resources now are focused on brown-skinned people, because only brown-skinned people can be terrorists in their eyes. I didn't hide my feelings about the racism I saw. I was working human trafficking. On one case I ran across a Pakistani woman who said the INS agent had raped her. I'd picked up enough of the language over there to get her meaning. The guy thought that no one would understand her, or believe her if they did. I asked him about it, to his face. He laughed, and though he denied it, I could see it in his eyes. I kicked his balls up so hard, I think his father felt it. He'll probably never have kids, thank God."

"You know, I went to prison for hitting a fed. A crooked one."

"So I read. Anyway, that wasn't real good for interdepartmental cooperation. I was busted down, and almost canned. Instead, they stuck me here in Maine, where there aren't many brown-skinned people, and where my career has gone to die. Guess they hoped I'd change my attitude, or the heat would die down, maybe in ten years or so.

"Joke was on them, though. I'm a damn good investigator, and started doing some digging, because I had all this free time. Guess what? I found out there was some truth to what the guy in Afghanistan had told me. But shadowy shit, you know, nothing solid. A piece here, a little something there. But you can add it up if you know what to look for. Anyway, I put together a report and sent it off.

"Came back two days later and I was told there was nothing to it, all stuff and nonsense. I was told in no uncertain terms that I should focus on other things. Said they'd even checked with the state department, and there was no truth to it. But I know that's shit. And it's happening here."

"Why wouldn't they be interested in that?"

"The Bureau doesn't deal with international geopolitics, only what happens internally. And much of what the Russians are doing here is either not technically illegal, or damned hard to prosecute. Hell, look at big companies, with industrial spying and hostile takeovers. Half of Wall Street and big banks are doing much of the same thing. We only get involved when they cross the line, and by then they're so entrenched, it's hard to bring them to account.

They're also pumping money into the American political system. They're buying or blackmailing people at all levels to advance their causes. Now that bribery is unrestricted and seldom tracked, we're getting sold out, piece by piece. Someday the bastards will own the President and the Senate, and then we little people in the good old U.S. of A are going to be well and truly screwed."

I rubbed my forehead. "Kind of hard to believe Maine is a battleground like this. Even a minor one."

She snorted. "Thing you learn studying history is that so many battles were fought in out-of-the-way places nobody cared about. Even the great ones. The tide of history has often turned because of what happened in some locale that most people couldn't find on a map. And Maine is out of the way, but it butts up against a country border that's easy to cross."

"Their governments are doing this?"

"No. Big-money conglomerates, with oligarchs who'll get major concessions and monopolies afterward. They use proxies, farm out all the dirty work. All huge, long-range moves, like I said. Major sums of money being shifted, thousands of lives. And all the nasty stuff and dirty players moving in that go with it, from places where there are people willing to commit atrocities. Like muscle from all the war zones; Serbs and Croats, for example. In case there are those who don't want to sell or roll over, and might need a little persuading.

"I tried to keep you out of this, told you it was above your pay grade. Because I've seen what they do to some who get in their way. Tortured beyond belief. But it looks like you've joined up now, my friend. So you are in the shit."

"What about you?"

She shrugged. "Not my first rodeo. And I signed up for it."

"Will the Bureau get involved now?"

"Oh, hell yes. That's why them coming at us was so important. A supposed accident, had it worked, was smart. They might have got away with it, especially with you in the car, with your background. We haven't been able to get anything prosecutable on them yet. Now I've got solid proof, can connect the dots, and can convince Washington this stuff is real. That means more resources. We've got a lever to move them with. If we can crank up the heat enough, maybe we can make them go elsewhere."

"How did Sprague figure in all this?"

"He was a bookkeeper at the paper company the Russians were going after. Don't know what he found, but it must have been good. I got an anonymous tip, and I'm sure it was him. He said he had some dirt, and he wanted to make a deal, because he'd stolen something. I was going to meet Mr. Anonymous the next day, but he never showed. They got to him first."

"That's why you knew I didn't kill him."

"You're just the poor doofus who got sucked into the jet engine."

"I might have been able to protect him, if I'd found him first."

She shook her head. "Don't take this the wrong way sweetie, but you're out of your league. You might have faced a gang, but this is an army. A well-armed, well-funded army of killers. You don't even carry a gun."

She had a point.

I sighed. "What's your next step?"

"Well, I have to take you into protective custody, don't I? There's a safe house we can stash you in."

I shook my head. "You think I'm going to sit around some house, twiddling my thumbs, while you're out fighting the bad guys? And for how long? Fielding said his cases can take years. Nah, that's not going to work."

A Darkened Room

"I *do* carry a gun. Don't argue with me."

Dale T. Phillips

CHAPTER 22

Before we got breakfast, Casey made us go back to the drugstore, where she picked up a few items of makeup. She spent some time in the car, using the visor mirror to apply a few things. When she was finished, with the big sunglasses on, you couldn't tell she'd been smashed up and driven over a cliff.

We found a diner, got a corner table away from other people, and both ordered huge meals. She'd popped more painkillers and had more coffee, so she was perky and talkative. About everything else but what I wanted to hear.

I interrupted. "Look, I know you don't want to tell me, it's an ongoing case and all. But who the hell are bold enough to go after the FBI?"

She swirled a spoon around in her coffee. "Russians."

"What? You're kidding."

"I wish I was. When the Soviet Union fell apart, Russia was still in the game. Some people there are spreading their tentacles again, seeing where they can influence things. But this time it's not political, it's money. The new god.

"When certain factions in a country have sucked their own neighborhoods dry, they have to go elsewhere for new opportunities. They look for easy pickings, places where there's not a lot of competition. Chunks of territory to control, on a world-wide scale. Billions at stake."

I drank my own coffee and thought about this. "A giant game of RISK, combined with Monopoly."

"Yup. So of course there's competition. When it happens, you can go head-to-head, or you can go sly and try a lot of back channels. So there's a thousand tiny battlegrounds, for little pieces of the pie. Butterfly effect. Put a little pressure here, cause a disruption there."

"Don't tell me Maine's one of those battlegrounds."

"It is. They're going after the lumber company that Sprague worked for."

"But why? Russia's got plenty of forests. They don't need Maine lumber."

"But Japan does."

I looked at her. "Russia and Japan in a trade war? Didn't they have a real war, about a century ago?"

"This one's all about the money."

Our waitress brought our food, and we dug in, pausing between bites.

I couldn't figure it. "So how does taking over a Maine lumber company hurt the Japanese?"

"One supply source cut off. Then another, and another. When the Russians have got the lumber all locked up, no more wood from the northeast. Multiply that times the other places they do it, and one day there's a real shortage back in Japan, resources harder to get. You either pay a lot more, work a deal while giving up major concessions, or go without. Soon it looks like their government doesn't get global trade. Shortages like that mean public scrutiny of government policies, and sometimes changes in government. Loss of confidence, even maybe a new election, with people more favorable to outside interests. Or just the threat of it, for leverage for better terms on some agreements."

"Wow."

"You saw some of that with Harada. There's more interest in North Atlantic fishing than you realize, more than sea urchins, and not just Maine. Japan's appetite is voracious, and they're competing to get all they can before the stocks totally collapse. Did you know that the cod off our shores were once so thick, you could almost walk across the water on them at some points? Now we've stripped the oceans dry, wiped out whole species of fish. It's just a question of time before they're all gone. So the Russians are moving in on the companies that sell to Japan. You of all people should notice the Japanese boats are no longer around Portland."

"Yeah, I thought they left because Harada was killed."

"In a sense, they did. His island was bought by a corporation that has so many shell companies, it's like those Russian dolls. *Matroishka*, I think they're called. But I'll bet you a year's salary if you get to the last one, it's got those Russian backwards p's. Same group going after Sprague's company. So many subsidiaries and shells to get through, but the heart is red."

"So the Russians are going after lumber and fish. What else?

She waved a fork. "Cars. The US is a major market for Japanese cars. Say there's one dealership that sells Japanese cars. Then a few other dealerships move in around it to sell Swedish, German, even American cars, at bargain prices. Nothing major by itself, but each taking a piece of business away, chipping away at the margins, until it's no longer profitable to sell those Japanese models in that location. Buyers have to go farther out, maybe decide to try something closer to home. Dealerships change hands or change what they sell. And it's happening across the country."

I put down my fork. "So they've got the world mapped out like a giant go board, with hundreds of pressure points. The Russians stake a position, like placing a stone on the board. By itself, it's nothing. The Japanese ignore it, or respond to it. Some points get hard fought, some are ceded without a struggle. But without opposition, soon there's a string of stones, a solid base."

She grabbed a forkful of hash browns off my plate.

I mused. "How'd you find out about all this?"

She sighed. "In Afghanistan, as Army Intel, we turned up a lot of weird shit, some of which you would just not believe. After the Russians left, there wasn't a lot of love for them. I ran across one old guy who spun me a tale about a war between the bear and the rising sun. Just like 1905, like you said. Maybe the Russians are still pissed about losing that one. I didn't believe it at first, and there wasn't much I could do about it anyway. We had other priorities, like staying alive.

"When I got back, I joined the Bureau. Most of our resources now are focused on brown-skinned people, because only brown-skinned people can be terrorists in their eyes. I didn't hide my feelings about the racism I saw. I was working human trafficking. On one case I ran across a Pakistani woman who said the INS agent had raped her. I'd picked up enough of the language over there to get her meaning. The guy thought that no one would understand her, or believe her if they did. I asked him about it, to his face. He laughed, and though he denied it, I could see it in his eyes. I kicked his balls up so hard, I think his father felt it. He'll probably never have kids, thank God."

"You know, I went to prison for hitting a fed. A crooked one."

"So I read. Anyway, that wasn't real good for interdepartmental cooperation. I was busted down, and almost canned. Instead, they stuck me here in Maine, where there aren't many brown-skinned people, and where my career has gone to die. Guess they hoped I'd change my attitude, or the heat would die down, maybe in ten years or so.

"Joke was on them, though. I'm a damn good investigator, and started doing some digging, because I had all this free time. Guess what? I found out there was some truth to what the guy in Afghanistan had told me. But shadowy shit, you know, nothing solid. A piece here, a little something there. But you can add it up if you know what to look for. Anyway, I put together a report and sent it off.

"Came back two days later and I was told there was nothing to it, all stuff and nonsense. I was told in no uncertain terms that I should focus on other things. Said they'd even checked with the state department, and there was no truth to it. But I know that's shit. And it's happening here."

"Why wouldn't they be interested in that?"

"The Bureau doesn't deal with international geopolitics, only what happens internally. And much of what the Russians are doing here is either not technically illegal, or damned hard to prosecute. Hell, look at big companies, with industrial spying and hostile takeovers. Half of Wall Street and big banks are doing much of the same thing. We only get involved when they cross the line, and by then they're so entrenched, it's hard to bring them to account.

They're also pumping money into the American political system. They're buying or blackmailing people at all levels to advance their causes. Now that bribery is unrestricted and seldom tracked, we're getting sold out, piece by piece. Someday the bastards will own the President and the Senate, and then we little people in the good old U.S. of A are going to be well and truly screwed."

I rubbed my forehead. "Kind of hard to believe Maine is a battleground like this. Even a minor one."

She snorted. "Thing you learn studying history is that so many battles were fought in out-of-the-way places nobody cared about. Even the great ones. The tide of history has often turned because of what happened in some locale that most people couldn't find on a map. And Maine is out of the way, but it butts up against a country border that's easy to cross."

"Their governments are doing this?"

"No. Big-money conglomerates, with oligarchs who'll get major concessions and monopolies afterward. They use proxies, farm out all the dirty work. All huge, long-range moves, like I said. Major sums of money being shifted, thousands of lives. And all the nasty stuff and dirty players moving in that go with it, from places where there are people willing to commit atrocities. Like muscle from all the war zones; Serbs and Croats, for example. In case there are those who don't want to sell or roll over, and might need a little persuading.

"I tried to keep you out of this, told you it was above your pay grade. Because I've seen what they do to some who get in their way. Tortured beyond belief. But it looks like you've joined up now, my friend. So you are in the shit."

"What about you?"

She shrugged. "Not my first rodeo. And I signed up for it."

"Will the Bureau get involved now?"

"Oh, hell yes. That's why them coming at us was so important. A supposed accident, had it worked, was smart. They might have got away with it, especially with you in the car, with your background. We haven't been able to get anything prosecutable on them yet. Now I've got solid proof, can connect the dots, and can convince Washington this stuff is real. That means more resources. We've got a lever to move them with. If we can crank up the heat enough, maybe we can make them go elsewhere."

"How did Sprague figure in all this?"

"He was a bookkeeper at the paper company the Russians were going after. Don't know what he found, but it must have been good. I got an anonymous tip, and I'm sure it was him. He said he had some dirt, and he wanted to make a deal, because he'd stolen something. I was going to meet Mr. Anonymous the next day, but he never showed. They got to him first."

"That's why you knew I didn't kill him."

"You're just the poor doofus who got sucked into the jet engine."

"I might have been able to protect him, if I'd found him first."

She shook her head. "Don't take this the wrong way sweetie, but you're out of your league. You might have faced a gang, but this is an army. A well-armed, well-funded army of killers. You don't even carry a gun."

She had a point.

I sighed. "What's your next step?"

"Well, I have to take you into protective custody, don't I? There's a safe house we can stash you in."

I shook my head. "You think I'm going to sit around some house, twiddling my thumbs, while you're out fighting the bad guys? And for how long? Fielding said his cases can take years. Nah, that's not going to work."

"I do carry a gun. Don't argue with me." We stood outside the diner. Now that I knew what was at stake, I wanted to do something about it. "So where do we go from here?"

She gave me a look with one eyebrow raised. "We go back to Portland, where you keep your head down, or preferably, take a vacation someplace far away."

"They tried to kill us. I'd like to do something about that."

"Lovely thought, but you don't have a badge, a gun, or a federal agency behind you. I do. There should be a car waiting for me back at the motel. I've got to organize a strike team down in Portland, and I can't watch out for you. I feel guilty about almost getting you killed, you know. Bad form for civilians to perish in FBI matters. It's on the news that we survived, so the ones who went after us may try again. So I need you out of the way, get it?"

My face told of my happiness without me saying it.

She went on. "This is my area. I've got the big guns, and I don't need you as collateral damage. Hate to be a bitch, but if you don't find a hole to hide in, I'm going to have to put you under guard somewhere in protective custody. Don't make me do that."

I put up my hands. "Okay, message received."

"Don't pout. I've got to go get my purse, which they recovered, and my new laptop. Then I've got to come up with a plan of attack by the time I get to Portland. Then I've got to scour this state for every damn person who might be connected to the bad guys."

"You're enjoying this."

"Knocking you down a peg? No. Well, maybe a little. But going after those bastards? Goddamn right. I've finally got a chance to do something about what's been going on. Now kiss me goodbye and wish me luck."

We went back to the motel. A man stood outside the door of our room, and another was behind the wheel of a Crown Vic, just in front. A second Crown Vic sat beside the first, with no one in it. Both men had the haircuts, suits, and the stone-faced attitude of feds. Casey went to speak to the outside man, who passed her a set of keys before getting into the first vehicle. She got in the second car and drove away.

I wondered when I'd see her again, realizing something profound. For the first time since Allison had left, I wanted to live again.

I went into the room to retrieve my stuff, and left the key there before going out to my car.

Back in Portland, I'd just got everything put away when my phone rang. I thought about not answering it, but picked up, just in case.

"Taylor?"

"Yeah," I replied.

"It's Warren Fielding." Ah, my favorite Treasury agent. "Saw on the news you had a little accident."

"If you can call someone trying to kill me an accident, then yeah."

Silence on the other end. Then a voice leaking obvious strain. "Please, for the love of all that is holy, tell me you were in Woodville only because of some hellish coincidence."

"Let me guess. You're running a case on the paper company."

Fielding was cursing, not very inventively. "We need to talk. Now."

I sighed. "Fine. Meet me at the parking lot at Back Cove. I'll be there in about twenty."

He hung up without further ado. I almost felt sorry for him.

Back Cove was a small body of water surrounded by the city proper. They had a lovely trail for walking, jogging, or bicycling, with exercise stations at various points. On good days you could see people windsurfing out on the water. It always recharged me to go there and absorb the air. After almost dying, I needed it.

Fielding was already there, and he watched me get out. We walked over to some benches, and sat looking out over the water.

"I should have known," he opened. "Of course when I have a big case, you're involved."

"Probably because when there's bad people doing funny things with money, there's a lot of ripple effect around them."

"Okay, so what do you have?"

"This going to be a mutual exchange?"

"As much as I can tell you."

"Okay. I was hired by a woman to look for her father, who was in some kind of trouble. They found him a couple day ago, murdered."

"Guy in the cabin up at Little Sebago?"

"That's the one."

He waited.

I went on. "Next thing I know, there's an FBI agent after me, because of something the guy had been involved in. I go up for the funeral, visit the company where the guy worked. A man there says the murdered guy took records and money from the company, which has affected the sale of the company. So he hires me to find the stuff.

"I go around town, asking about the murdered guy, and nobody wants to talk.

Someone put the word out that he screwed everybody, and that the sale might not happen because of what he did. Some guys jumped me in a bar over it, but the FBI agent came by. Next day, she and I are in a car that got rammed over a cliff."

"Who did it? Any idea?"

"Well, come to find out, there's Russians involved. They've got some deals going on cross the state."

Fielding sat back, jaw hanging open. "Sonofabitch. I'd heard rumors… but."

"Yeah. Apparently, they want to buy the company, so they can cut some of the timber supply to Japan. Part of some great chess game, a global struggle for resources and power."

Fielding shook his head. "How in the hell do you find this stuff out? We only recently got onto it."

"Pull one tiny thread, and next thing I'm in a bigger mess than I could have imagined."

"Jesus. Same here. We got wind of a certain company doing a major buyout in Maine lumber. They're just a shell, part of a spiderweb of companies we've been tracking. And yes, the trail leads right back to some Russian-based interests. We figure they also want to launder millions by taking the company over. Great place to bury costs and cook books. Unless we can get something hard on them, it could go through, too.

"And then I get a cryptic phone call, telling me I should take a close look into the company books and the sale."

I thought it over. "You think it was Sprague?"

"Unless someone else wants to nix the deal."

"Seems most people in town are for it."

"They've been struggling for years, like so many other places. Lot of people see it as a way to keep going, but it's rarely the relief they hope for. The assets get stripped, people get canned, and the gates are closed six months later. Then the town dies. But to them, any hope is better than none."

"Why do you think Sprague contacted you?"

"He's one of the accountants, must have found something in the records. Either on the company side, or the buyer's side. Knew there were shenanigans."

I grinned. "Shenanigans?"

"Fine. Something criminal going on."

"So he takes the books, grabs some expense money, and goes on the lam."

It was Fielding's turn. "On the lam?"

"You're not the only one who can use funny words."

Fielding nodded slowly. "He lets authorities know enough to check into the sale, hides his information in a safe place, but he's killed before he can release it."

"People start checking, and someone gets overly nervous. Tries a hit on the FBI, probably to stop the investigation."

Fielding shook his head. "Big mistake. That's asking for nuclear-level blowback."

"Not if you get away with it. Accident."

"The FBI takes care of their own. You bet they went over that accident site with every lab tech available. If they find the vehicle that hit you, they'll drop the hammer hard."

"I hope so. We barely got out."

Fielding sighed. "I'd like to go in there and take everything connected to the sale, but I can't yet. Not enough evidence for an audit. I can go to a judge and connect the dots, but without anything solid, they won't allow it. An anonymous tip that says something is up just isn't quite enough."

I wrote Casey's number on a scrap of paper from my wallet. "Here's the agent in charge. If I see her again, I'll tell her we talked. Maybe you can pool resources, work together, share information."

Fielding snorted. "You have no idea how government agencies work, do you?"

"I would hope they would cooperate on big things."

"Not a chance."

"Make the call anyway. Tell her I said it would be a good thing."

Fielding laughed. "Right. She'll probably tell me to go fuck myself."

CHAPTER 23

I dropped in on Miriam to see how she was doing, and greeted Theo.

"Are you all right?" Her look of concern was intense. "I saw on the news."

"Just banged up a little," I said.

"Was it something to do with my father?"

"I doubt it," I lied. "Just some yahoo in a truck hitting us, then taking off so they wouldn't get in trouble."

"Did you see who it was?"

"Didn't have time. Wham, bam, over and done. How are you two getting along?"

Miriam smiled at Theo. Best houseguest I've ever had. Very considerate."

Theo bowed his head at the compliment and smiled.

"I feel safe with him here," she said. "I was pretty shaken up after what happened."

"Then if you don't mind, I'd like him to stay for a couple more days, just until things sort out."

"What things?" Miriam was frowning.

"The investigation. Did you know your father's company was being sold?"

"No. That would have upset him. He worked there for years. It was his whole life."

"But everything's okay here?"

"Yes, no problems."

But over Miriam's shoulder, I saw Theo shake his head in the negative. Uh-oh.

"Would you like some coffee?" Miriam seemed eager to play hostess, and it would give me a chance to talk to Theo in private.

"That would be great, thank you."

She went off to make the coffee, and I raised my eyebrows at Theo.

"Somebody's watching," Theo said. "Brown sedan. Parked up either end of the street from time to time. I'd go confront them, but didn't want to leave Miriam alone. She and I went to the grocery store, and we were tailed. Whoever did it was good, couldn't get a vehicle make for sure. But I knew they were there. Same cars driving by too often, a blue Buick LeSabre and a dark green Ford."

"Jesus," I said. "Some operation, if they've got that many people and cars. They out there now?"

"I looked, just before you came. Not there."

"So they know you're here, and they're keeping watch. I think I'd like to talk to whoever's in that surveillance car. Next time you see them, call me. I'll surprise them."

Theo gave me a serious look. "That really an accident, someone hitting your car?"

"No, they were gunning for us. Almost worked, too."

"So you think it would be a great idea to sneak up on some potential killers, with no gun."

"Good point," I said. "What do you suggest?"

"If you're okay with them knowing we know, I'll call the cops next time. Doubt they'd dare shoot a cop in the daytime for a routine check."

"I'd call my FBI lady, but she'd probably lock me in a cell. For my own protection, of course."

"Sounds like you two are getting along just fine."

"She's here in Portland putting together a strike force. That might rattle some cages."

"Might make whoever's watching do something more than watch."

"That's what I do, on a bigger scale. Yeah, it's dangerous. Does Miriam have someplace else to go, just for a few days?"

"Go where?" Miriam set down a tray with three coffee mugs, a sugar bowl, and a small cream pitcher.

"Someplace else. Safer."

"Why wouldn't I be safe here? Is something going on?"

"People at the company could find out where you live. If there's more who are angry like the guy who was at the service, I'd like you to be somewhere else."

Miriam frowned. "There's more to it that you're not telling me."

I took a deep breath. "The people that think your father took some money when he left the company might come looking for it."

She looked scared and unhappy. I felt like crap, but didn't know what to do.

Theo was at the window, with a curtain aside just enough to see out of. "They're back."

I looked up. "Brown sedan?"

He nodded.

"Screw it. I'm calling Casey."

Miriam had stopped crying and was looking from Theo to me and back again. "Who's back? What's going on?"

"Yes?" Casey's voice came over the phone.

"It's Zack. Listen up. Miriam Sprague has someone watching her house. She's been followed, and several crews are doing surveillance and drive-bys. Tell me it's not you guys."

"Not us."

"Then it could be the bad guys, and if so, they may be armed. I don't want anyone getting shot. Can you spare a couple of agents to ease in and see who's in that car and if they have a connection?"

She cursed. "Thought I told you to stay away from this?"

"I'm just seeing how Miriam is, and was told about this. You've got the address. Brown sedan, parked up the street. Your guys should spot them in a heartbeat. You going to check it out?"

"Sure, I've got nothing on my plate for this afternoon."

"Hey, I called you, instead of Portland PD."

"We're on it. Can you not do anything stupid for fifteen more minutes?"

I hung up. Theo had explained some things to Miriam, and her face was a mask of worry.

Ten minutes later, the fun started. I looked out the window, and three cars had boxed in the brown sedan. They pulled a guy from inside, and had him with his hands on the car roof while they frisked him.

Twenty minutes later, I got a call from Casey. "We've got a hit. Mike Peters, born Mikhail Petrovich, out of Boston. Carrying a nine-millimeter, but he's fully licensed, courtesy of the Acme security firm down in Fall River."

"Acme?" I chuckled. "Somebody been watching old Roadrunner cartoons?"

"Vehicle's registered to Bob and Sarah Johnson, with a Portland address. Mean anything?"

"What's the plate number?"

She read it off.

"That sounds like the same one from Ozzie and Harriet. Odd couple from the service for Sprague."

"Well, I'd certainly love to have a chat with the Johnsons. Seems they also own a large black Chevy pickup."

"You don't say? Funny world."

"We've got a BOLO out for them, and are watching their place. We're getting a warrant to search it."

"You folks sure work fast."

"When we want to. Hey, thanks for the tip."

"Don't mention it. Just glad to move things along."

"Okay, but back off now, you hear? Things could get messy."

"They always do."

Dale T. Phillips

CHAPTER 24

About five minutes after I got back to my place, the phone rang. I sighed and answered.

"Is this Mr. Taylor?"

"The one and only."

"Norris Deschene here. Find anything yet?"

"Well, the FBI just nabbed possible Russian agent outside of Miriam Sprague's house."

"Jesus."

"You calling just to check in?"

"No. The cabin up at Little Sebago, where they found Sprague's body. Can you take me there?"

I figured out what he wanted. "You want to look for what he hid."

"I've got a metal detector. Worth a shot."

I told him where to come get me. Might as well earn my pay.

Deschene was dressed in jeans, a flannel shirt, and work boots. He drove up to Little Sebago, obeying the speed limit. Some people in Maine still did that.

"I saw on the news about your accident," he said.

"No accident. Deliberate attempt."

"Jesus. How'd they find out who you were?"

"I was asking around town. But it might not have been me they were after."

"The FBI agent?"

"Maybe."

Deschene swore. "This has certainly gone tits up. Things were quiet two weeks ago. But I did warn you, right?"

"Not worth the pay, frankly."

"Never is, when things go wrong."

"So you're just going to look around the place, and maybe go digging?"

"Unless you have a better idea."

I didn't.

"And if that doesn't work, Winslow had a friend somewhere along the lake. Bert Everly. I haven't been able to find an address, and there's no telephone number, if he even has one. Perhaps you could ask around, find out where his friend's place is, in case Winslow left the records there."

We got to Sprague's cabin, and saw the crime scene tape back up on the door. It felt like someone had trickled ice water down my spine. The memory of finding Sprague came back, and I reeled a little.

Deschene stood with a metal detector in his hands. "You okay?"

"Yeah, just dizzy."

"Look at the beer bottles and cigarette butts. What's that about?"

"No idea."

"Since we can't get inside, let's look around. Check for any patches of earth that look differently-colored from the ground around it. I'll fire this baby up."

Deschene put on headphones and adjusted some knobs on his device. I scanned the ground, checking for any discoloration. Deschene made long, slow sweeps with his detector. After a bit, he pulled off the headphones. "Got a hit."

He marked the spot, and went to his car and brought back a long-handled spade. He put the tip into the earth and stepped on the back of the blade, slicing into the ground. I watched him for a few minutes. He stopped and mopped his brow, breathing heavily.

"Want me to take over?"

"That would be great," he wheezed. I didn't want to see him get a heart attack. I'd have a hell of a time explaining that one.

I dug for a few minutes, feeling like I was looking for buried treasure, like playing pirates as a kid. I hit something with the spade. "Got it."

Deschene took the shovel and slowly scraped away some dirt, and probed around the edges of the thing in the ground. After a little bit, he was able to get the spade underneath it and leverage it up. I saw a rusty cube with the sides gone, about the size of a breadbox. Maybe a little bigger.

"What is it?"

"Junk," he said, almost spitting the word. "Useless damn junk. Why would someone bury this in the yard? There's nothing in it."

I shrugged.

"Well, back to it," he said, and exchanged the spade for the detector. He started his sweep once more. I resumed scanning the ground, but looked up to see a cop car come to a stop.

Ah, shoot.

I tapped Deschene on the shoulder. He lifted the headset off one ear, looked where my finger pointed, and nodded. He took off the headset.

A young cop walked toward us. "Hands where I can see them," he said. What are you doing here?"

I thought it looked pretty obvious, but I let Deschene do the talking.

"Hello, Officer, I'm Norris Deschene, head of security for Woodville Paper, up in Woodville. Winslow Sprague, who owns the cabin here, was our employee, and he left with some items of ours we'd like returned. I'm afraid he may have hidden the items here on his property, so I thought we'd take a look. Since he's deceased, we didn't feel there was any harm."

"You can't just come here and do that. You can't just walk onto someone's property and dig it up."

"It looks like other people have been using this place."

The cop looked disgusted. "Yeah, a murder, big news for around here. So people come to gawk. Reporters, curiosity seekers. Damn kids, who come out to party, smoke, drink, screw, look at the death house, take some pics. You're the first ones digging for buried treasure, though. I should charge you with trespassing."

"Officer, I'm sorry, I didn't think we were doing anything wrong."

"Let me see some ID."

We handed him our licenses, and he went back to his car and called on his radio, after looking at the license plate on Deschene's car. We stood for a few minutes. I felt foolish and exposed, and wondered if the dispatcher would tell the officer to shoot me, considering my history with local law enforcement.

The cop came back and handed us our licenses. "Your lucky day. I'm not going to charge you, but if I see you out here again, you're getting arrested. Understand?"

"Yes, sir," we both said.

"Now get out of here and don't come back."

In the car, I began to breathe again. Another close call. I was a little too near the fire of getting myself behind bars once more.

But I couldn't let it go. When I got home, I called Peggy, an artist I'd met on a previous case. She was not happy with me chasing Allison away, as she'd had a crush on her, but she'd somewhat forgiven me. She had a talent for combing through records to find obscure information, and I wanted her expertise. She knew I paid well, and as an artist, she could always use the money.

After the preliminaries, I told her about Sprague and Bert Everly. She said she'd look into it. I wasn't sure if I was helping myself, or getting in deeper.

CHAPTER 25

On the way back to Portland, my mobile phone rang. I was hoping for good news, for a change.

"Zack, it's Theo. They grabbed Miriam."

"What?"

"Woman at the door. That threw me, I was less suspicious. She stuck a gun in my face, a man came in after, also waving a gun. They zapped me with a Taser, got me face down on the floor. Miriam ran out the back, the woman yelled something, and they took off after. By the time I got up and out, they were gone."

"You okay?"

"Yeah, shook up, but not hurt. If Miriam hadn't run off, they might have killed me, so I couldn't identify them. I'm calling the cops."

"No. I'll call the FBI instead." I disconnected and punched out Casey's number.

Casey answered. "What is it now?"

"They grabbed Miriam. The Russians."

"God-damn it!"

"Woman and a man. Waving guns, had a Taser. Zapped Theo and took her."

"Fuck, fuck fuck!"

"Think it was that couple? The Johnsons?"

"They're really going off the rails. I should have seen it coming."

"What do we do?"

She sounded angry as hell. "Christ, I don't know. They'll torture her until they're sure she doesn't know anything, then kill her."

My mind was churning, and the guilt wanted to overwhelm me. "I've got an idea."

"I'm all ears."

"Our names were all over local news after the accident, so they know who I am. They're probably staking out my place, too, since they're clearing the board. So use me as bait. With luck, they'll take me to the same place they took her. Makes sense. You swoop in and grab them before they carve us up."

"You're a civilian. I can't take that chance. What if we lose them?"

"Look, I'm not real keen on this, but we have nothing else. We know they're desperate, so time is short. I'm in it now, root, hog or die."

She swore again. "Fine. I'll set things up here." She gave me an address to drive to. "Hope you're ready for this," she said.

I doubted it, but there wasn't any other real choice.

I stopped by some office buildings. Casey led me past a desk and a guard. She flashed an ID badge at the guy, and nodded toward me. "He's with me."

"You gotta sign in, Miz Selkirk, you can't just…"

She ignored him and streaked past, me close on her heels. She passed by the elevator and ran up a flight of steps. She went into an open office, and there were three men arguing.

"We don't have any time," she cut them off. "This is Zack. He's going to wear the transponder, and we're hoping they grab him and lead us to the other hostage. Assume armed and deadly, but I want them alive."

They looked at each other, then at Casey. One raised an eyebrow. "Flashbangs?"

I chilled at the thought of a couple of flashbang grenades going off near me, but Casey shook her head.

"No, straight in. Tasers and beanbags, instant knockdown."

They nodded, and Casey turned her head to one of them.

"Barry, get him rigged."

Casey and I followed Barry into an inner office. Barry held up a small device. "It's not a mike, just a signal beeper to tell us where you are."

I took off my shirt, and he did a double-take at the mass of scar tissue on my torso. "Holy shit."

Casey looked me in the eyes as a wide grin spread on her face. "Sorry, cowboy, no wire, nothing worn. They might search you."

I frowned. "Then where?"

"Let's just say we're going to grease it up good first. I'll leave you boys alone."

I looked at Barry, who had an apologetic air. He now had on a latex glove, and the device was enveloped in a condom. All at once I got it. Damn feds. "At least it's small," I said. "Let's get this over with."

A few minutes later, we rejoined Casey in the other room. I didn't sit, trying to adjust to the uncomfortable position of the small device. She grinned at me a moment before going serious again. Men wearing Kevlar vests and tactical gear and carrying weapons stood in the hall. One big guy held a portable battering ram, the kind the cops use when raiding a crack house. Casey had a vest hooked over one arm.

She rattled off the address of my apartment. "That's where we'll start. If they take the bait, that is, Zack here, we follow discreetly. I'll take lead vehicle, so constant radio contact in case I need others to switch. Our channel, not police band, since they're certain to monitor that. We've got the transponder, but don't lose them. We don't know how far they'll go. I don't want to use the helicopter, that's a dead giveaway. We wait five minutes, and charge in. They'll likely shoot back if we give them a chance, but I want them alive. Any questions?"

There were none, and with my life on the line, I was impressed that they knew what they were doing. Grim-faced professionals, going into a situation where lives were at stake, including their own. It almost made me like the feds. Gingerly, I walked down with them all. In the lobby, the guard looked like he wanted to further discuss Casey's breach of protocol, but one look at the entourage, and he wisely sat back down. Outside on the sidewalk were three black SUVs and a cab. Casey pointed to the cab.

"That's Sid. He's with us. He'll take you in."

I nodded, my heart thumping like a steam engine. Everyone was getting their gear into vehicles and not paying attention to us. Casey leaned in and grabbed my lapel. "When we come in, hit the deck and stay alive."

I couldn't speak. I eased my way into the back of the cab. A few minutes later, we pulled up at my apartment.

"Good luck," said Sid.

I got out and tried not to look around as I headed for my apartment. The cab drove off and things got quiet. I sensed the two guys coming up behind me, and then something hard poked me in the side.

"You will come with us."

I turned my head to see a swarthy man with beard stubble. He pressed a pistol against me. I'd play it like I wasn't expecting this.

"Who are you? What do you want?"

"Shut up. You come."

"You can't get away with this," I did my best attempt at an outraged sputter.

"He said shut up," said the other one. "Or I hit you. Get it?"

I nodded, and slumped my shoulders. They led me to a car around the corner. One pushed me into the back seat while the other pointed the pistol at me and got in front. He stayed twisted around to aim the gun at me while the other one drove. The driver spoke into a cell phone. It sounded like Russian. I was pretty sure I heard a '*da.*'

"Where are you taking me?"

No response. Not a talkative bunch. I wondered how well they'd maintain the silent act when facing twenty years in prison for kidnapping and conspiracy.

We drove out near the airport and stopped at a row of buildings. The driver got out and took out his pistol, training it on me while the other one got out on his side. They kept a distance, both with guns on me, and indicated a door. I opened it and saw a third guy holding a gun, and a few feet away, a very frightened Miriam.

Dale T. Phillips

CHAPTER 26

One of the thugs kicked a chair over to me. "Sit."

I did, and another one grabbed my wrists, pulled them behind me, and I heard the rip of duct tape. I felt the strips go on, wrapping around, binding my wrists together. He came in my field of vision to look at me and held up the roll. "You talk out of turn, I tape mouth? Got it?"

I nodded. I looked at Miriam but didn't dare to even ask her how she was. Her head was down, but she didn't look like they'd roughed her up yet, a good sign. The three men with guns looked over at the other man, who rolled a tool cart over. He was tall and skinny, balding, and he smiled to show a mouthful of crooked yellow teeth. His fingers were stained with nicotine.

"I am Yakov," he said. "And we need to know things. I will ask you questions. If you tell us truth, all is good. If not, I must persuade you. I have asked her a few things already. If you lie, I will know, and will hurt you both. Do you understand?"

I nodded, widening my eyes in fear. It wasn't an act. I hoped like hell the transponder was working properly.

Yakov brought over another chair and set it facing me. "Now then." He reached into the top tray of tools and took out a set of pliers. They had stains on them that probably weren't rust. He smiled, and clicked them together a few times. The guy looked like he really enjoyed his work.

He opened his mouth to say something, but was interrupted by a loud bang as the door blew open, with FBI agents pouring through. The three thugs whirled and reached for their pistols. I heard loud pops, and something smacked into the thugs, making them jerk like puppets. Then I heard loud crackles, and two of them fell, twitching violently. The other was on his knees, also twitching, and I saw the wires connecting him to the end of the Taser held by an agent.

Yakov's mouth was wide open, and I was disgusted at the sight of those awful teeth. He held his hands up, still gripping the pliers. Two agents with guns grabbed onto him, and slammed him down to the floor before they cuffed him. I started breathing again.

A woman agent bent over Miriam, speaking softly. Miriam was crying, but she stood up and went with the woman. Casey stood nearby, surveying the situation. She appeared satisfied. She came over to stand in front of me.

"You okay?"

"Uh, yeah, I guess. You guys are good."

"Damn right. We have to be."

"Can someone cut me loose?"

She shrugged. "I don't know. I kind of like you helpless. Harder for you to get into trouble like that." She gave it another second and laughed. She took out a folding knife and snapped the blade open. I had an uncomfortable echo of Yakov with the pliers, but she went behind me and cut the tape. I pulled myself free of all the sticky bits and rubbed my wrists.

"Now what?"

"Now you get taken to a safe house while we work over these mooks."

"And Miriam?"

"Someplace else. Boston. Farther away. She'll be safe down there."

"I can't go back to my place?"

She shook her head. "Nuh-uh. They might have a B team."

"They won't get bail, will they?"

"No way in hell. Federal court, flight risk, ongoing investigation. I'll be checking with Interpol and would bet my car they've got warrants out somewhere else."

"What if they cut a deal? It's happened to me before."

"They're Russians. They never talk to the law, never give anybody up. They'll go down and do as much time as they're given without a peep. But we're going to have a run at them anyway. I've got a long night ahead." She patted my cheek. "You did good."

"Thanks. One more thing."

"What's that?"

"How do I get this damn gizmo out of my ass?"

Sid drove a Ford LTD this time, and took me to Kennebunkport, just down the coast from us. He told me the house had been used by the Secret Service for a time, since the presidential Bush family had a compound just up the road. It was a rare show of cooperation

A Darkened Room

between agencies. I had him stop at the little bookstore in town before we got there, and picked up a handful of books to read.

I called Theo and asked if he was okay, and told him Miriam was safe. I felt guilty about putting him in harm's way, and he felt guilty about having Miriam snatched while he was guarding. Circle of blame.

It was strange to be so inactive after all that excitement. Once my mind had settled down and put the thoughts of Doctor Torture out of my head, I started reading, while Sid prowled around peeping out windows from behind the drapes he'd drawn.

The day wore on as I read. I finished one novel and started another. Sid, my babysitter, sat in the other room and watched television. He phoned for a delivery pizza for our dinner.

At about ten o'clock, Casey knocked on the door, and entered with a couple of paper bags. She told Sid he was off for the night, and to be back at eight the next morning. She locked the door after he left, and set an alarm on a panel. She removed her suit jacket and sat at the dining room table. She took a pair of chicken sandwiches from the bag, and a paper container of French fries. She unwrapped a sandwich and bit into it. She wiped her mouth with a napkin.

"Want some?" She asked between bites.

"No thanks. We got takeout pizza earlier."

"Good. I'm starving," she attacked the sandwich and rapidly devoured it. She chomped fries as she unwrapped the second.

"So what happened?"

"We did our thing, put them in individual rooms, and let them know how many years in a federal pen they were looking at. They sat like statues and only asked for an attorney."

"They get one?"

"Not a chance. Special cases, they're on ice. The attorney would have just been a messenger, let the boss know exactly what happened. Now maybe the bossman will be wondering where his boys went. As I suspected, they've got records. Two of them are ex-military, Yakov's a war criminal, don't know how they snuck him into the country. We weren't getting anywhere, so we put each of them in solitary to contemplate their sins overnight. We'll go again tomorrow, but I doubt we'll get anything. Maybe we can find out about their organization from their movements."

"So what now?"

The second sandwich was gone, and she shook the bag of fries into her mouth for the last of them. She crumpled the bag up and took a bottle of champagne from the second bag. "Celebrate, dammit. This is the first real break we've got. They went at us, we smacked them down hard. Took out their active soldiers. Grab me a glass."

I got up and went to the kitchen for something for her to drink from. I returned with a tumbler. "Sorry, no champagne flutes."

"This'll do." She'd popped the cork on the bottle already, and poured herself a glass of bubbly. She took a very healthy swig, and burped loudly.

"Sorry," she said. I smiled back. She drank some more, as I gathered up the wrapping and napkins and stuffed all the trash into one of the paper bags. She finished the glass, and poured another full one.

She was grinning. "Any trouble getting the transponder out?"

"Very funny. I hope to not have to do that again. How long do I have to stay here?"

She looked into her glass. "Dunno."

"I'm not taking up permanent residence while this case drags on."

She looked up. "You got something against living?"

"Sitting in here for a long time isn't living. It's not much removed from another kind of jail, although I'm sure you'd feed me better."

"Safest thing to do would be to relocate you permanently, somewhere far away."

"You know that's not going to happen."

"I guessed as much." She poured another glass.

"You going to finish that whole bottle?"

"What are you, my mother?"

"Maybe I could think of something else to do."

"Is that so?" Then she shook her head. "What am I saying? I told you this wouldn't happen again."

"I know. I'm a distraction."

"Goddamn right you are."

She got up and came over to stand next to my chair. She bent down and placed her mouth on mine. The sweet taste of the champagne brought back conflicting memories, but I pushed them aside, and focused on the sensation of her mouth. She broke off the kiss, breathing a little faster. "Damn you."

"We can take it slow."

She roughly grabbed my hand. "The hell we can."

CHAPTER 27

With Casey gone the next morning, I was ansty. Sid was still my keeper, but I wanted to be out on the hunt for these people who had stirred up a giant hornet's nest. Cooped up in the house, I exercised and did some kata, formalized karate routines. That and meditation kept me busy for a few hours, but then it got boring. I rarely watched television, so I read some more. I finished another book. I looked out the window a lot, despite Sid telling me not to. A person in a window is a target, after all.

I wasn't allowed to go back to my apartment, in case it was being watched by more of them. This house had towels and all that, plus toothbrushes and basic toiletries, like soap, shampoo, shaving cream, and disposable razors, but someone had to get me clean clothes to wear. This was a problem, as Sid said that policy was that an agent must be at the safe house at all times. I joked that they didn't want me having a party on government property while he was gone. He wasn't amused. Sid phoned in my request for clothing, along with an order for some Chinese takeout for our dinner.

At dinnertime, an agent came by with takeout and a bag of clothes for me. He'd got it mostly right, but I really hated this new thing of having other people shop for what I wore. We ate our dinner, and Sid chatted about his boyhood in Massachusetts. He'd been on his high school baseball team, and clearly wanted to relive those days, or talk about the Major League teams, especially the Red Sox, but I didn't have much to add. I wasn't about to get into my sordid past, so we made conversation as least awkwardly as we could.

A few hours later, Casey returned, and gave Sid the rest of the night off. She looked tired. She went to the cupboard and took out a tumbler. At the table, she opened a bottle of wine she'd brought.

"Anything to eat? I'm starving."

"You got wine, but you didn't even stop for food?"

"Essentials."

"We've got some leftover Chinese. The Bureau was generous tonight."

"Thank God."

I put it on a plate and heated it up for her while she drank some of her wine. I brought it to her along with a fork and a napkin. She attacked it like she hadn't eaten all day, which she probably hadn't.

I wondered if she'd had any luck. "Any progress?"

She poured more wine. "We've got jack shit. Bastards won't say a word. We even paid for a translator, all for nothing. Got a report on the shotgun. Nothing usable, dammit."

"Who bought it?"

"Sprague himself. A week ago, at a sporting goods store. Probably thought it would protect him. Autopsy on Sprague didn't show anything, so they were pros. That means a lot of money is involved, but we don't know where or how much is happening."

"So what's next?"

She pushed her plate away and poured more wine. "We'd love to find whatever Sprague took. A set of books, a thumb drive, a CD, whatever. Might be the lever we can use to crack them open. But without it, we're still stumbling in the dark."

"I was trying to find him, not something he hid. Maybe I could help with that."

"Thanks for the offer, but no. If I haven't stressed this enough before, you are not to go anywhere near this. It's an official Bureau matter now. We have policies and procedures to follow. Rules of evidence and all that. You breaking into a place, for example, could ruin a case, taint any evidence we found."

"What about using me as bait again?"

"They weren't expecting it, so it looked easy. Won't be like that again. And next time, they might be pissed at losing a couple of soldiers, so they might just shoot you instead of grabbing you. And there you are, without even a gun, not that it would do you much good."

She finished the last of the wine in her glass, and looked at the empty vessel like she was wishing it would magically refill. "And I've found you useful in other ways, so I want you alive and kicking."

"About that. Do we need to talk some more?"

"You mean like how I'm breaking all protocol and risking my career because I'm banging a potential witness?"

"Well, no, I was thinking more like us, and where we stand. But yeah, I don't want you in trouble because of me, much as I want to keep seeing you."

She reached over and pinched my cheek. "What the hell, I might not even live through this, so I don't care much about the impropriety."

"I hope you don't mean that."

"I'm the only one pushing this agenda. These buggers play for keeps, and if I bollix up their plans too much, they might decide to remove the liability, take another run. They tried it once, remember."

"Would you do me a favor and please start wearing your vest full time?"

"Can't. Makes me look fat."

I opened my mouth to admonish, but she laughed and cut me off. "Kidding. Yes, play time is over, and I'm going to go around, strapped, packed, and ready. But for right now, I'm going to take a shower."

"Need any company?"

She gave me a long look. "I might, at that."

Dale T. Phillips

CHAPTER 28

The next day, I was getting really twitchy. Casey and I had enjoyed another great night together, but I didn't like the fact of her being in danger and spending long hours hammering away at this case while I sat on my ass trying to keep busy. How long would I have to stay here? I didn't know my limit on absolute boredom. My lengthy hospital stays after injury had tested those limits, but at least I'd had Allison to keep me company. Here I was just a nighttime booty call. Not a role I was comfortable with.

I prowled the rooms like a restless big cat in a zoo. I exercised until I was exhausted, showering and thinking about escaping to go for a run. But I didn't want to get Sid in trouble, even though he kept telling me to stay away from the windows.

It was late afternoon when I gave another sneak peek and saw a vehicle pull into the driveway. It had a cable company logo on the side, one of those magnetic slap-on signs. The driver stayed put, and a guy with a clipboard got out. He was a big guy, hair cropped short.

I called to Sid. "We've got company. Don't answer the door."

"What is it?"

"White panel van, can't tell if there's someone else in it. Driver's still behind the wheel, and there's a guy with a clipboard coming toward the door."

"Something about them?"

"You didn't call the cable people, did you?"

"No." He eased his .38 from his belt holster and kept it by his side. The doorbell rang. Sid breathed more rapidly. "Might be nothing. I'll check."

"You wearing your vest?"

He unlocked the top lock and started to turn the doorknob when bullets crashed through the door. He fell back, and I took off into the house as the big guy smashed his way in. I remembered the back door was locked, too, and it would take extra time to undo that. I'd likely be shot before I got out. Instead, I grabbed a kitchen chair and stepped back, timing my swing to catch the big man who charged into the kitchen. I connected well, and followed with a hard kick to his groin, pushing the chair up under his chin as he bent forward. I let go of the chair and grabbed for his gun hand, twisting when I had a grip. He cried out and dropped the gun, and I gave him a palm strike under the chin that snapped his head back into the door jamb.

I'd have hit him some more, but I was outlined in the doorway, and there was another man at the front door. Three shots rang out, and the guy jerked as his face exploded into a red mist. Now I raced for the back door, and got that lock opened and leaped out. I'd no sooner hit the ground when another big guy with a baseball bat came from somewhere and swung at me. I rolled away, and he grunted and came after me. I got to my feet, grabbed a trashcan and stuffed it in his face, pushing him back. He fell, and I took off. In a fight like this, I didn't know how many there were, or where they were, so getting away was the only option. My only mission was to not get caught.

I was practically doing parkour in my efforts to escape, leaping over or bouncing off obstacles, trying not to be a stationary target, throwing a roll in when there was an open space. No bullets flew after me, and no sounds from assailants, but I didn't stop until I was sure.

I sucked in air, the adrenaline still coursing through my system. I realized they'd tried to take me alive, which explained the mook with the bat, instead of a gun.

As I stood hunched over, recovering, with my hands on my thighs, a man came out of his house. I realized I was in his backyard.

"Who are you? I thought I heard shots."

"You did. Call the police."

He went back indoors, and I followed him. He frowned and tried to bar my way, but I put on my mean face. "Those men were killers. Call the police, and then I have to make a call to the FBI."

He blanched and pointed to the phone. I grabbed it and punched out the emergency number. I gave rapid instruction when I'd got the dispatcher.

"Units are on the way," came the female voice. "Please stay on the line."

"Can't," I said, and disconnected. I called Casey's line, mentally urging her to pick up.

"What?" It was her.

"Attackers at the safe house. I got away, but they shot Sid. Don't know how he is, but he shot back and got one. There were at least two others. I ran."

She swore. "Where are you?"

I had my wind back, and my anger. "Not dead or caught, and I want to stay that way. You've got someone on your team who gave them the location. Your people are compromised. I can't risk it. I'm going off on my own."

"NO. Stay where you are. We can keep you safe."

"I'll call you," I said, and disconnected. I had to make one more call. Luckily, I knew the familiar number.

"J.C., it's Zack. I'm in deep shit. I just escaped an FBI safe house in Kennebunkport, because some shooters came after us. I got away, but the bad guys got hold of FBI insider information, and found us. I need to hide out, but the cops are going to be all over this place. I don't have my car. Can you come down here? They might let you through with the others if you use your press pass to investigate the shooting. At least you'll get close enough for me to find you, even if they cordon off the immediate area. I'll try to get to you."

"On my way," he hung up. The good thing about having friends who've been through some serious shit is that they don't stop for lengthy discussions in the middle of an emergency. They do what needs to be done, and save the explanations for later. Right now, I needed a quick way out of this town, as it was too easy to seal off.

I was getting afraid of how quickly things were escalating.

CHAPTER 29

"Thanks," I said, slipping into the passenger seat of J.C.'s car. It had been a harrowing game of hide and seek, with me slipping through the police in a small tourist town.

"It was a little sudden," he said.

"What did you get me into? This is about Miriam's father."

"What's going on?"

"A global struggle for trade."

"What? Who?"

"Russians and the Japanese."

"What is this, 1905?"

"They're fighting a giant chess game over resources, hundreds of actions. Maine is apparently one tiny battleground."

"Jesus Christ. How does Miriam's father fit into this?"

"Russians were buying the company. He found out something, took the financial records, and some money."

"And how did you find out?"

"The FBI. Agent Selkirk discovered I'd found Winslow's body. You know when I was up in Woodville, the Russians tried to kill us. They were watching Miriam's house, and we called the FBI to grab one of them. They attacked Theo and grabbed Miriam. I went back out as bait, which they took, the FBI followed, and we got her back. That's when the FBI stashed me in the safe house. Miriam's somewhere else. But the bad guys just tried again."

"All that? I just saw you three days ago."

"I know."

"I cannot believe this."

"An hour ago, I saw a guy's head explode. Before that, I was pinned to a chair and a Russian torturer was about to use pliers on me. It hasn't been fun."

"Good lord. Looks like we're clear. Where do you want to go? New Zealand?"

"Let me make a call first." I clicked off and rang Peggy. "Hi, kiddo. Got anything for me?"

"Yup. Had to check county tax records to unearth the address, and went on from there. Bert does not have a phone, his driver's license is expired, and he lives alone on the lake. The road to his place is private, gated, and marked with No Trespassing signs."

Considering how vigilant the local cops were, I didn't want to risk driving around the lake and getting caught where I'd been told not to be. I'd have to figure something out.

"What's the address?"

"It's one of those dirt lake roads, not signed, damned hard to find. Stop by, I'll show you on a map."

J.C. stopped by Peggy's place, and I greeted her.

"Heard you were in an accident," she said. "You okay?"

"It was no accident, and no easy out. For the moment, I'm okay. But I'm in some pretty deep shit. You heard about that body they found up at the lake?"

"Yeah, I wondered if this was connected."

"A guy from Sprague's company said a friend lived near him on the lake. Sprague had taken something and was hiding it. I'm wondering if this guy knows anything."

"It's not far. A few hundred yards." She unrolled a detailed map. "See? Here it is."

"And there's Sprague's cabin." I squinted and looked closer. "What the hell? Doesn't look like there's a road connecting the two."

"There isn't. The road ends. You have to go around the lake to get there, on the other side."

"He gets a place near his friend, and can't even go visit easily?"

"Zack, they're on a lake."

"Oh. Right. Yeah, Sprague had a canoe."

"Probably paddled over."

I thought it over. "I could do that. Would help with the patrolling cops, too. I got rousted the last time at Sprague's place. They probably don't patrol from the water side as effectively." I looked back at the map. "How would I know which one it is, though?"

"I got a picture from the realtor. Here. It's got a small dock, and has green shutters. Big shed next to it."

"Fantastic job, Peggy. Here." I took out my wallet and gave her a hundred-dollar-bill, the secret one I had stashed for emergencies.

"Zack, that's too much. I did about two hours, tops."

"You know how handy it is to have someone be able to research things while I run for my life?"

In the car, J.C. did not look happy.

"You're on the run from Russians and the FBI, and you just want to keep going, is that what I'm hearing? Do your usual charging around?"

"Pretty much."

"What about laying low for a while?"

"The Russians are on a tear, so everyone's in danger. They have to be stopped."

"Won't everyone be looking for you?"

"I've got to do something. Maybe I can find Sprague's records and help Casey to put out the fire we started."

"Bad plan."

"Only one I've got. Oh, I need to borrow your kayak again."

He gave me a look like that wasn't going to happen.

I stared back at him. "This is where I work on your guilt for getting me into this whole mess."

"Low blow," he said.

"Sorry, but I'm running out of options."

Dale T. Phillips

CHAPTER 30

My mobile phone rang once more.

"Taylor, it's Norris Deschene. Our expedition was cut short last time, but I know the records are somewhere around that cabin. I can feel it. Come with me. I need you to watch for the cops."

"Gosh that sounds so tempting, but I've just survived another attempt on my life, and I'd love to catch my breath."

A space of silence. "If you find what Sprague took, you can put a stop to them, you know."

That might actually be true. "Still have to beg off."

Deschene sounded almost offended. "I'm paying you a lot of money."

"Not enough."

"How about another thousand?"

I sighed. "Fine. Let's take your car, in case the cops grab us and impound it."

"Fair enough."

He picked me up a few minutes later, and we drove up to Little Sebago.

"This wasn't what you were driving last time," I said.

Deschene grinned. "Just in case that cop is still hanging around. Didn't want him recognizing my ride."

"What will you do if he comes back?"

Deschene rubbed his thumb and first two fingers together. "A little baksheesh takes care of everything."

"You're going to try to bribe him?"

"Why not? He's a country cop. Probably doesn't clear thirty thousand a year. I give him the next two mortgage payments, he'll probably help us dig."

"Not everybody has their price, you know."

"You did," he gave me a look.

Good point. I knew this whole caper had very little chance of success, but I also had little else to go on.

We got to the cabin with no sign of the local constabulary. I had the spade, and Deschene had his detector in hand. "I'll do a good sweep, and you keep your eyes peeled for any visitors."

I nodded, but a flock of birds burst from a nearby tree like black shrapnel into the sky. I frowned, and felt an electric jolt go through me.

"Down!" I hit the dirt and tried to will Deschene down.

He looked at me, and his head exploded in a red burst. The rest of him collapsed on the spot.

I crawled behind a tree, gulping air. I looked around, but there was not enough cover in the yard. If I ran, the shooter would cut me down in a second. I was pinned down, trapped. No way out.

"We meet again," said a voice, close by. I recognized it as Ozzie, the man from the parking lot. "You have been a hard man to kill."

"Bob Johnson, I presume?"

His tone came out sharp. "How did you find my name?"

"Your friends at the warehouse gave you up."

"You lie."

I kept silent.

"No matter. Our little game is at an end."

I tried for a delaying action. "You killed Sprague out here."

"Of course."

"I know where the books are that he took."

He laughed. "We don't care, you fool. We don't want them found. That's why we left him as we did, so things would quiet down. Without them, there is no further investigation, and the sale can still go through. You have been quite a nuisance, trying to stir things up. That's all over now."

My mouth was dry, my mind reeling with the thought of my imminent death. I realized how much I wanted to live, despite my sorrows. A little too late.

Another voice from not far away. "Police. Drop the gun!"

I heard a loud crack, and poked my head out. Bob Johnson had dropped his rifle, and clutched his throat, which poured red onto his hand. He fell to his knees, and toppled over. Mere yards away stood the young cop that had rousted us before, still in his firing stance. He straightened up, his face twitching with different emotions.

A few minutes later, the cop still looked like he was in shock. Shooting someone knocks your psyche down.

I'd called Casey, and the cop had called his people.

"You did good," I said. "He was a Russian assassin. He killed Sprague in this cabin."

"I know. I heard."

"He'd have killed you. And then me."

"Yeah."

"You've got damn good reflexes, or instincts, to pop off on an armed killer. You serve?"

"Tour in Afghanistan."

"There was nothing you could do. Another second, and he'd have shot you."

His voice sounded far away as he remembered. "He was turning, bringing it up."

"How'd you get so Johnny-on-the-spot, anyway?"

"I figured you two would be back at some point. Been keeping an eye out. Came through the woods to catch you in the act. Heard the shot, heard you two talking."

"Thanks for my life."

He looked up, surprised, then nodded. I hoped it would help.

"If you've got someone at home, they're going to be very glad you did what you did."

He didn't respond, and I heard the faint wail of sirens. I looked at the bodies of Deschene and the man who called himself Bob Johnson. Too many had died over this deal.

Dale T. Phillips

A Darkened Room

CHAPTER 31

We were at police headquarters in Portland. I wasn't sure if anyone was watching us through the one-way this time. Sergeant LaGasse looked amused, probably figuring he'd finally get to lock me in a cell. Lieutenant McClaren was seated across the table. Two ranking state cops and two suits were also present. Casey was barking orders at someone over the phone. She'd looked at me like she wanted to fry my ass in oil, but I hadn't had a chance to talk to her in private.

I sat with my arms crossed, waiting for my attorney. In legal matters, he was Superman, constantly battling to keep my dumb ass out of jail. With him in the room, it would be harder for the police to ensnare me, or for them to anger me enough to say or do something really stupid. He could produce anger at will, and his ire was impressive and scary, his pronouncements sounding like an old-time revivalist tent preacher, carrying the word of a vengeful god. His impeccable attire, height, and flaming red hair made an imposing force for others to contend with. I'd left him a message with a brief explanation of what had happened.

Parker came in and greeted everyone, set his briefcase on the table, and folded his hands over his stomach. I began to relax.

"Now how can we help the Portland police?"

"Counselor," greeted Lieutenant McClaren. "Your client was involved in yet another shootout."

Parker raised his eyebrows. "So is this a voluntary, cooperative information session aiding your investigation, or an attempt to get him to say something that you can charge him with?"

"He was caught trespassing on the murder site yesterday, with the deceased. Digging up the yard, looking for something. He was warned to stay away. He returned, with the deceased, and now we have two more bodies."

Parker nodded. "So are you planning on charging him and the deceased with anything?"

McClaren didn't look embarrassed, as he'd been down this road many times before. "Counselor, you know how we work. You see that we're not even recording this, so you know we're not likely to charge him. But yes, we'd love to know more about why Mr. Taylor was digging around a murder site with another man who was murdered there."

Parker looked at me.

"Deschene said he wanted to look at the place, and was paying me. He wanted something that Sprague had taken from the company. We looked around that first time, didn't find anything, and were told to leave by a local officer. Deschene took me for a ride today, drove me back there, and next thing he was dead and the killer was about to shoot me."

One of the state cops spoke. "Where do you know him from?"

"I met him when I was up in Woodville, at the paper company where Sprague worked."

"And why were you out there with him?"

"He hired me to help find the stuff Sprague took. He called me that first time, and I showed him to the cabin."

"You find anything?"

"Didn't have a chance. We got out, and boom, he was gunned down."

Parker spoke. "I understand there's a witness who can corroborate. An officer."

"We have his statement."

"As you do my client's. Ms. Selkirk, do you have anything to add?"

She sighed. "This is one hell of a mess. But it's the FBI's mess from here. We'll be handling Mr. Taylor from now on. He'll be available for further inquiries."

The police in the room looked at each other, but there was nothing they could do. Feds trumped locals and state every time. She was pulling rank, but they were used to it. They shuffled out, leaving me, Casey, and Gordon.

"Counselor," she said to Gordon. "I'm Special Agent Casey Selkirk. Pleased to make your acquaintance. You have a formidable reputation. I hope we never have to meet in court as adversaries. Although with Taylor as a client, you never know."

Parker laughed and shook her hand. His voice was pure melted butter. "Agent Selkirk. Thank you for coming to the rescue."

She nodded. "I explained a few things to the local cops. They wouldn't have believed him."

"His explanations get lengthy and complex, so your intervention probably saved him a thousand dollars."

"He won't have a chance to get into any more trouble. I'm taking him into protective custody."

"No," I said. They stared at me. Casey was eyeing me as if covering me with ice.

"Look," I said. "You had me in a safe house, and they knew I was there. That means someone in your office told them. You've got a leak. I'm not being set up again."

"They'll kill you."

"If they know where I am. On my own, I can keep away until you round them up."

"No. It's too risky."

"You get rid of the leak, I'll reconsider. But I don't trust your people until that happens."

She opened her mouth to argue, but Gordon interrupted. "Agent Selkirk, it appears your organization has been compromised. I suggest you turn your efforts to finding out who is responsible. Mr. Taylor is aware of the risks he is taking, and accepts them. He wishes to remain at large. Should you insist on curtailing his freedom, and anything happens to him, you realize you will be liable for prosecution yourself."

She turned to Gordon and gave him the full-force glare. He gave it right back, unruffled.

"Fine," she almost spat. "Let the dumbass get killed, then."

I wanted to tell her how sorry I was, but she spun away and was gone.

Parker eyed me. "Little history there?"

"What do you mean?"

"Please," he said. "Are you too stupid to see that she cares for you?"

CHAPTER 32

A short dock, green shutters, big shed off to the side. I'd found it.

I let the kayak drift, remembering when I'd paddled out to Sprague's cabin and discovered his corpse. A body found like that stays in your memory, and the ugliness of it crops up to remind you at odd times. I'd seen too many dead bodies, and was tired of it.

Had Sprague left anything here? Could I find the key that would solve the puzzle? Or was it just another phantom clue in the demise of a man who had worked for many years along the straight and narrow, only to meet an ignominious end in a dark cloud of suspicion?

I took a few strokes and glided to the dock, reaching out to catch, and eased the kayak against the wood. I got out and tied off, looking at the cabin. I walked to the end of the dock and stood, waiting to see if anyone would come out.

Someone did. A man who looked to be in his seventies, white hair, glasses. Faded shirt and worn pants.

"You lost?" The accent was pure Maine. *Ayuh*.

"Are you Bert Everly?"

"If you're here to sell me something, go away."

"I'm here about Winslow Sprague."

Since he was only a few yards away, I saw him blink rapidly. "What about him?"

"Miriam wanted me to find out what happened to him. You know her, right?"

He nodded. "Met her once, long time ago."

"Can we talk?"

He looked at me for a long moment. And then another. "Come up to the porch."

I followed him up. He eased himself into a rocking chair, and I took the only other seat, one of those Adirondack chairs that I could never get used to, as the balance was too far back.

He started rocking and gave me a good scrutiny. "What's your name?"

"Zack Taylor."

He didn't offer any hospitality, including his hand to shake, so I didn't, either. He seemed the typical crusty old Yankee, suspicious of strangers.

"How'd you find me?"

"Norris Deschene, from the Woodville company, mentioned you were a friend living around here. You, ah, are harder to track than most people."

"Like it that way. Worked with Norris 'til 'bout seven, eight years ago. How is he?"

"I'm afraid he'd dead."

Everly stopped rocking and sniffed in surprise. "Well ain't that a shame. How?"

"He was murdered."

Everly looked somber, his brow lined.

"As was Winslow," I added.

He nodded. "Knew he didn't do it himself. Never was the type."

"I'm sorry about your friend."

He shook his head and started rocking again. "Ain't right. Either of them. Here I am, only a few months left, and they go first."

I raised an eyebrow.

"Cancer," he almost spat the word. "Hurts like fury. Hell of a way to end."

"Sorry to hear it."

He waved a hand. "Had a good run. No family left, purt near everyone I knew is gone already. Can't drive no more, half blind, hurt all the time. Just want to be left alone." He gave me a glare in a sudden flash of anger. "And here you come, telling me about people getting murdered? What do you want?"

"I'd like to see to it that the people who killed Winslow and Norris are caught."

He stiffened, and stopped rocking once more. "You some kinda cop?"

"No, but I poke around in a useful way sometimes. Miriam wanted me to protect her father, but someone got to him before I did."

Everly started his motion again, back and forth. "I knew something was up."

He'd seen Sprague. My pulse took off like a race car. "He came by?"

"Ayuh, stopped in for a visit. He was troubled some. Said the company was selling, but they'd diddled some books for a time. Was gonna screw everybody. I worked there, too, didn't think that was right."

"Did he leave anything with you?"

Everly cast his gaze to the side quickly, a glance at the shed. "Nope."

He was lying. It was why I watched people's faces and bodies when asking them questions, because many weren't good liars, and had what poker players called an easy tell, a giveaway to know when they were or were not being truthful. Everly's tell let me know I really wanted to check out the area, most likely that shed.

"Shame," I said. "He had some things that could put this whole business to rest, help the police catch the ones responsible. Norris was looking for whatever Winslow had, and he was killed by the people that also wanted it."

I was dangling bait, but he didn't take it. Instead, he tried for nonchalance.

"Well, he didn't stay long. We talked old times for a few. He was gonna retire soon, finally fix up his car--" He coughed, maybe to cover up whatever else he was going to say, but it sounded bad anyway.

"You okay?"

"Just dyin' is all. Don't even got enough for a proper burial."

I looked at the cabin, figuring he could sell this place, if he needed money.

He saw my look, and shook his head. "Built this place with my own two hands, twenty-eight years ago. I'll be damned if I let anybody else move in, like some damn flatlander Yuppies. Burn it to the ground first."

"Anything you want me to say to Miriam?"

"Her father was a good man. 'Bout all there is to say."

I took a deep breath and gave it one last shot. "There's some people thinking Winslow took something he shouldn't have. I'd like to clear his name."

His mouth was pinched, the lips close-set. "Well, good luck with that."

"You can't help me?"

"I don't know you from Adam. You show up on my dock and tell me bad things, and want to go pokin' around."

"Is there any way I could get you to trust me? Maybe bring Miriam by?"

The anger again. "I don't want no more goddamned visitors, unnerstand? Just leave me alone. Get in your little boat and paddle away from here, and don't come back. I got a shotgun inside, and ain't afraid to use it."

People get nastier as a defense mechanism when they are backed into a corner. I got to my feet and left without saying anything further.

But I'd be back, shotgun or no shotgun.

CHAPTER 33

I called Theo, who seemed in good spirits, all things considered.

"All better?"

"Yeah, just wounded pride. I opened the door because it was a woman. Just let her stick a gun in my face. Stupid."

"If it's any consolation, you got off lucky. They blasted into the safe house and shot the FBI agent with me. He's okay, was wearing a vest, thank goodness. Even got one of the attackers. So if you hadn't opened, they might have tried shooting first. And we got Miriam back, so all good. Sorry about the whole deal. Didn't think they'd react like that. These guys don't care about fighting the FBI."

"Who the hell are they, anyway?"

"Russians."

"Get out."

"I mean it. Some big group of international players is having a giant game, and we're one of the arenas."

"No shit. That's wild."

"With all that's happened, they've lost some soldiers, have to be hurting. And now Miriam's out of reach."

"But you're still rolling back and forth like a duck in a shooting gallery."

"Yeah," I said. "Still some unfinished business."

"I know that line. You want some more help."

"I do, but I'm still feeling guilty."

"Do I have to get shot this time?"

"Probably not. The guy said he has a shotgun, but he's old, and half-blind, and it'll be dark. So you're probably good."

Theo laughed. "Worst part is, you're absolutely serious."

"Yup."

"Okay, tell me what great plan to get me killed you've cooked up this time."

Hours later, I'd paddled to a spot on the lake not far from Everly's cabin. Tree branches hung down over the water, providing a hidden spot where I could tuck in and not be seen, while I waited for nightfall. Fresh batteries were in the walkie-talkie I carried in a plastic bag, to prevent it from getting wet. I was slathered in insect repellant, and had brought some sandwiches to eat while I was waiting. I ate, and drank some water as dusk turned to twilight.

When I judged it safe, I went ashore and carefully picked my way through the undergrowth. I was wearing long sleeves so I wouldn't get scratched as I moved along, and I carried an empty knapsack with a large capacity. There was enough cover to conceal me, but not so much that it required a machete to get through. I took my time, glad that there were no other residences in this stretch. Everly's hermit predilection was helpful in this case.

I made it to Everly's cabin, and lay low until I saw the lights go out when he went to bed. I gave it another half-hour, and thumbed the switch on the walkie-talkie, the volume set to minimum.

"Go."

"Roger that," came Theo's voice.

Up the road, he would be getting out of his vehicle to walk down the gated road and approach the cabin on foot. I'd be breaking into the shed while he watched from a distance. If Everly came out, Theo would warn me and start a ruckus to distract Everly while I made my getaway. Not a complex plan, but simple was usually better.

Of course the shed had a padlock on the rolling track door. I could pick simple locks pretty easily, but just try it in the dark sometime. I spent some time and a lot of cursing before I got it open. There was no noise from the cabin. Old things being rarely opened usually made a hell of a racket, so I reached up and sprayed the bejeezus out of the track apparatus with a can of WD-40 that I'd brought. Gently, I slid the door open just enough to squeeze through, wincing at the creaking rattle. I gave it some more spray and slid the door shut.

Using a small penlight I carried for nocturnal missions such as this, I flicked it on with the beam pointed down. A quick scan of the shed's interior explained why Everly had been so prickly and private.

Marijuana plants stood along a wall. I smiled. He likely used the pot to alleviate his cancer pain, but the stuff was still illegal, and he didn't want to spend the last of his life in jail. No wonder he was so hard to find, and didn't want company. Well, his secret was safe with me.

The big item in the shed was a tarp-covered object. I lifted a corner of the tarp to see a Ford Thunderbird from the nineteen-sixties. What once might have been a beautiful ride was now a falling-apart bucket of rust, with faded paint.

All the doors were locked. I used the focused light to peer through the windows, but saw nothing. I went to the trunk and got my lock-picks out again. This went easier than the shed padlock, and the trunk lid opened with a protesting creak, even after my generous coating of the hinges with more WD-40.

An old blanket was spread in the back, and my heart sank. But I moved the blanket aside, and nearly cried out for joy. My heart was thumping, and I might have been a little unsteady. After such a time of turmoil, was this the secret treasure? The thing Sprague had been killed for?

Two duffel bags. I used my kerchief and opened the first, and there were ledgers. A pile of them. No doubt they were the cooked books. Without leaving fingerprints, I quickly riffled through a couple, and knew I'd struck the mother lode. Records of withdrawals, names, transactions. The paper trail of the company misdeeds. Evidence to bring down the real thieves, and maybe bring an end to the Russian involvement and this stupid game.

The second bag made me happy, as I gazed at stacks and stacks of money. Tens of thousands. Sprague's getaway stash, retirement, whatever. I unpacked the duffels and repacked them into my knapsack. I gently closed the trunk without too much sound, and replaced the tarp.

My walkie-talkie hissed. "Porch light just came on. He's coming out."

"Shit. Commence Operation Drunken Loony."

I crouched in the dark as I heard Everly's voice. "Who's out there? I know you're there."

Music erupted from Theo's boombox. I peeked out the slit in the door, and saw Everly shine a flashlight down the driveway. He was carrying a shotgun. He walked toward the sound, as I pushed the door open a little more and eased out.

"Turn that shit off," commanded Everly. What the hell you doin' here?"

I've been given my window of opportunity, and had closed the door and relocked the padlock. Theo turned the sound down. "I'm looking for Jackie's camp," he slurred, as if he was drunk. "Is Jackie there?"

"There's no goddamn Jackie here. You got the wrong damn place. Didn't you see the No Trespassing sign, you damn fool?"

"I wan' see Jackie. Tell her I'm here."

"I told you, she ain't here. Now get the hell out."

"A'right, a'right. I'm going."

As Theo backed away up the driveway, I faded into the bushes in the other direction, with what I hoped was a way to end the mess.

Dale T. Phillips

CHAPTER 34

Theo was at the lake landing, headlights on to show the way. We got the kayak loaded onto his car and drove back to Portland, laughing about our adventure.

"Thanks for keeping me from being shot," I said. "He had me for sure."

"Yeah, nice of me to offer myself as a big, black target."

"I told you, he can't see very well. And you could have hid behind that boombox."

"In the future, let's cut down on the numbers of guns being waved, shall we?"

"I'm all for that. This should make up for all the trouble." I set down a stack of a thousand dollars on the console between us. Theo glanced at it.

"Almost worth getting shot, the way you pay."

It was late, but the fenced-in storage facility in Westbrook where I had my unit was open twenty-four hours a day. I signed in at the gate for the sleepy attendant.

Theo stayed in the car while I went in to where I had a nice little safe with a pair of motion detectors on it, bolted to a sheet of metal underneath. If anybody did discover my treasure box, they'd have a hell of a time getting away with anything. The metal sheet would have to be cut to move the safe, so they'd need special tools, time, and the ability to ignore a piercing alarm. You could go up to the safe and bang on it, but any more than that, and a shriek of unearthly clamor would erupt. It wasn't foolproof, but it would do. The place could burn, and my safe would still be there, the contents intact. I could come here any time day or night, see if anyone else was around, and go to my private place.

My pirate heart warmed to see the tidy little stacks of money filling the shelves of the safe. Everly would get a surprise package of a few thousand dollars, with a note of thanks, supposedly from Sprague. Miriam would get the lion's share of the rest, with enough left over for my expenses and legal fees, and a little more besides.

Among the financial records was an envelope with Miriam's name on it. Inside was Sprague's letter to Miriam, which ran several pages.

My Dearest Miriam,

Let me explain what happened, and why you may not see me for some time.

I worked for Woodville for thirty years, since back in the sixties. Saw them through all the lean times. Now with most of my friends and neighbors gone, I'm turning sixty-five, and the company is pushing me out the door, in advance of the sale. They think to save a little by doing so, but it will cost them much more.

Remember two years ago, my heart attack, when the overwork and stress got to me? That hospital stay and recovery took all my savings and more. The company insurance didn't cover everything, and I still owe over twelve thousand dollars. I never told you, because I didn't want you to worry.

I'm an accountant, so why didn't I plan for retirement? Well, I did. We had a pension plan, and I was in it from the start, thirty years' worth. The house was paid for, so I was all set, I thought. I wanted to restore old classic cars when I retired.

Because of the sale, I went through some old records. I found out the pension fund has been repeatedly raided and "adjusted," to the point where I'll get a miserly eight hundred dollars a month. Bastards stole the rest. Their names are in the records, including five senior company officers still here. People I trusted and worked alongside of.

They were getting fat bonuses to reduce head count ahead of the sale to some out-of-staters. The parent company has no sense of loyalty, either to its employees or the state of Maine. The old Woodville used to do responsible foresting, replanting trees to replace what they took out. The new company doesn't feel that's cost-effective, so they'll just cutting everything as fast as they can, selling it out of the country, and let the devil take the hindmost. If nothing is done, there'll be thousands of acres of clear-cut like ugly bald patches across the state. The soil will wash away, the ecosystems will suffer disasters, and no one cares, apart from a few occasional protesters. The politicians won't speak out, afraid of criticizing the company and "losing jobs." Hah. We used to employ hundreds, and provided a good living for Mainers. Now it's just like the fishing industry, where they gouge the resources until there's nothing left, and pull out after everything collapses.

Seeing what they'd done and what they were doing, I got scared, then I got angry, and then got greedy. I took some money, what I thought was rightfully mine, and I took some of the records, which showed how they ripped off the pension fund. I went on the run, and tried to contact you, even though I didn't want to put you in any danger. I'm working on a plan to get them off my back, which is why I have all the information ready to drop to the authorities.

I'm getting out of this, and to hell with all of them.

So now you know. If anything should happen to me, I'll make arrangements for you to get my money, so you will never have to worry.

Love, Dad

I sighed. I didn't think I'd be turning in this particular portion of Sprague's revelations. I wanted the money I'd found to remain a secret, as well as Miriam's. Otherwise, the money would go into the system as evidence, and get tied up in courts until it disappeared completely. If you think I'm exaggerating, read *Bleak House* by Charles Dickens to find out what happens to a large fortune that is pecked away to nothing, year by year, by multiple people dipping their beak.

I thought I'd type up an edited version of this, just as an explanation, and pass it off as his final letter, so she could get closure. It wouldn't be the first time I'd done a little discreet forgery to save someone some heartache.

Dale T. Phillips

CHAPTER 35

In the morning, I went to one of those strip-mall copy stores, and spent some time and money to have a few sets of copies made of some of the records. I had a fake letter from Sprague, leaving out the part of him taking money along with the records. Then I drove to my storage unit and packed one set away, and dropped another set off at J.C.'s, along with a short explanation. J.C. said he would write up the story, and clear Sprague's name. I knew he'd do a great job of telling the truth. And Miriam would know, if I could get word to her. She might just be out of danger soon.

Then I called Casey.

"Where the hell are you?"

"Nice greeting," I said. "Sid okay? I saw him go down."

"He's fine, his Kevlar stopped it all. What trouble are you in now?"

"None," I said. "All peachy-keen. You find out who was the leak in your organization?"

"Yes, the Russians got to him, had some juicy blackmail. He flipped and told us everything. Our roadblocks have been effective, and we've arrested their other soldiers. Looks like their organization here is crippled. You can come in now."

"Good thing, because I was going to suggest it. You'll never guess what I found."

"Hopefully, a way to stay out of jail."

"Better. I have Sprague's financial records. The ones he took from Woodville. You can start the wheels of justice."

"You'd better not be playing a joke."

"I swear. You'll be able to tell exactly what happened, and who's responsible. I'd like to bring them to your office."

"Excellent plan. I may not arrest you."

"Great. Be there soon."

I called another number.

"Fielding."

"You know that case we discussed? How would you like a copy of the financial records Sprague took from Woodville?"

Silence on the line.

"You still there?"

"I'm here," he said. "If you're dicking me around…"

"I'm not. I have them, with a set of copies for you."

"I might almost forgive you for everything."

"One thing."

"I knew it."

"You have to share with the FBI."

"That's not how we do things."

"Maybe not, but you'll have to on this. You both have interests, so I'm sure you can sort it all out."

"How do I get these records?"

"Come on down to the FBI office." I gave him the address. "I'm on my way."

A short time later, I watched as Casey and Fielding eyed each other like opposing cats. Casey scanned a sheet of paper she'd pulled from one of the two boxes I'd put on her desk. "This is a copy. Where are the originals?"

"Safe. I want to make sure nothing happens to them. This will get you started."

She opened her mouth to object, but resisted.

"Both agencies have vested interests in this. You can work together and call a big win for interagency cooperation. Much better than a pissing contest of jurisdiction. Dawn of a whole new era."

Fielding shrugged. "I can deal with that."

Casey grinned. "Our brass always wants all the credit. I'm going to have a hell of a time explaining why that's not going to happen."

"After you explain that you cracked the whole organization in this state, they should cut you some slack."

Casey was eyeing me suspiciously. "How did you get these?"

"I have my ways."

"You broke in and stole them from somewhere, didn't you?"

Fielding laughed, and she glared at him. "What's so funny?"

"Biggest gift horse to come your way, and all you want to do is check the mouth."

"We have laws and procedures for gathering evidence."

"So do we. But this asshole just goes out and does whatever he does and drops it on us like manna from Heaven. We'll make something up in the reports. We always do."

Casey looked like she wanted to say more, but made a face. "I'm going to get someone to log in this evidence."

After she left, I looked at Fielding. "So am I back in your good graces?"

"Are you kidding? You just gave me years of work. I'll never get to leave Maine now."

"What about your career?"

"Oh, now you're concerned for my career? After you almost single-handedly sunk it."

"Consider this a peace offering."

Fielding studied the remaining box, a duplicate set of the records for his agency. "Wasn't there some money taken as well?"

"I don't know anything about that. If there was some, and it's recovered, it should probably go to Miriam."

"After it goes through the system."

"Which could take years, if it ever gets to her."

"I see. Well, I hope it finds its way to her."

"I've got a feeling it might."

"Of course you do."

I had the uneasy feeling Fielding knew too much about my finances. I thought about the safe, and the tidy stacks of bills, and wondered what he would do if he knew about it. I hoped I'd never have to find out.

Dale T. Phillips

CHAPTER 36

The tornado of events had blown through, and left a path of destruction in its wake. I was happy to have a couple of days when no one was trying to kill me, to catch up on my rest. I went to a Schooner Fare concert, and heard the trio sing folk songs and sea shanties, which did much to clear my head and drive some of the images and memories away for a while.

I sent money to Bert, supposedly from Sprague, and had a bag of cash for Miriam when she returned. Whether or not she declared it on her taxes was up to her. Some of the money I kept for myself.

Casey called me one night. "You, me, dinner, one hour. Dress code, very nice. I'll pick you up."

"What if I already have a date?"

"Ditch her, or I'll shoot her. But you don't, so stop playing."

She picked me up, looking spectacular in a black, floor-length dress.

"Wow," I said.

"You don't look so bad yourself."

"Where are you taking me?"

"Someplace nice."

Indeed it was a lovely restaurant. J.C. would have approved.

"Mind if I get wine?" She grinned at me. "Might improve your chances of getting lucky."

"Then by all means, go for it."

"We're celebrating. Four of the senior staff of Woodville Paper were arrested for their financial misdeeds. Deschene would have made five, but the Russians saved us the cost and trouble of a trial."

"What does that mean for the company?"

"It was already limping along, hoping for a Hail Mary buyout. Someone may still come by, but the current deal is dead and gone. Treasury will go after the Woodville Four, and by seizing their assets and trading payback for some time off the jail sentences, a good portion of the pension fund might be recovered for the workers. Had the deal gone forward, they'd have got very little. So Sprague really did save their bacon."

"Doesn't sound good for the future of the town."

She nodded. "Sad story, too often told."

"How goes the fight with the Russians?"

"We won this round, but it goes on, just not here for now. We turned the heat up, and they scattered like rats. Maine is now lost to them, scorched-earth, so they've cut their losses. We executed a number of warrants in a dozen different places, and shut down their entire theater of operations in the state. Fielding seized assets: houses, cars, bank accounts, and we grabbed records. We moved so fast, they didn't have time to shred them. We've got every other group from ATF to the SEC wanting a piece of the pie. Not counting the international groups."

"Congrats."

"They won't see daylight again until they're too old to do much but sit in a wheelchair."

Casey sipped her wine and smacked her lips.

"And we found the truck they drove us off the road with. Paint chips from my car still in the grill."

"I'm glad you got closure on that."

She looked around. "They needed so many extra people, they sub-contracted out some of the work. And guess what? Those folks aren't as loyal as the home-grown soldiers. We've got two of them flipped already, giving us more evidence and witnesses."

"So does this mean you're going to have more time, or less, for nights with me?" I had all my hopes set on a positive answer.

The skin around her eyes softened, giving her a look of sadness that wrenched my heart.

"The outstanding success of the operation is our downfall. They're moving me to Boston, and I'll only be up from time to time for the trials. This is our last night together. I leave day after tomorrow."

My mouth went dry, and I couldn't speak. She was going away, after filling the empty space within me.

She looked at me intently. "Hey, I thought you'd be relieved."

"You haven't had enough wine to believe that."

She shrugged. "Thought I was a little too much for you."

I took her hand. "You are. And I'm grateful."

She looked thoughtful. "You know, Boston's not that far away."

Much later that night, in spite of being happily tired, I felt my mind going down darker and darker paths. It was quick and overwhelming.

Casey noticed. "Why so sad?'"

"You saved me, revived me. When you leave, I'll be empty again." I shuddered as I thought of Sprague, sitting in that chair, in that lonely, utter stillness of a darkened room.

"The knight killed the dragon, and now he's got nothing to do? No more sense of purpose?"

"Something like that."

She nodded, and ran her hands over my scars, the red ridges and holes and discolored patches. "You need the fight. There are more dragons out there, you know. Find another one, you'll find your purpose."

I grunted. Maybe she was right.

"There's a reason you settled here, Zack. Did you know Portland's city seal shows a phoenix rising from the ashes, with the motto Resurgam?"

"I will rise again."

"Yeah, you will." She kissed me, and then giggled as she moved her hand lower. "In more ways than one."

THE END

Dale T. Phillips

LIKE MORE ZACK TAYLOR?

Sign up for my newsletter to get discounts on upcoming titles
 OR- Get a free ebook or audio book
 At http://www.daletphillips.com

A MEMORY OF GRIEF

Read on for the first chapter of *A Memory of Grief*, the first book of the Zack Taylor series.

CHAPTER 1

Pain can be nature's way of telling you that you have done something really stupid. So I was getting quite a lecture. There was no way I could have won the fight, and sure, I'd known that going in. But I gave it my best. Then came the kick to my head, so fast that I had no time to block or duck. For the next hour, I'd simply tried to reassemble my thoughts.

Now I sat on a barstool, aching down to the bone with bruises and stiff limbs, holding an ice-filled bar towel against the cut over my eye. The coolness felt good. My head throbbed, but by some miracle I didn't seem to have a concussion, so I counted my blessings.

We were at a private nightclub near the edge of Miami's Little Havana. At Hernando's Hideaway, I was in charge of security, taking care of whatever trouble came up. Here in Miami, there was always trouble.

The mirror behind the bar showed the reflection of people around me. Hernando had permitted my rooting section to come in with me, even though the place didn't open for another few hours. The pain took all my focus for the moment, so I didn't want to talk to anyone. But I couldn't ignore Esteban, watching me from behind the bar.

"Your face looks hurted, Zack. Are you okay?"

I wasn't, but I didn't want to worry the kid.

"I'm fine."

"Want more ice?"

The water dripping down between my fingers had gone tepid.

"Sure."

He took the wrap from me, shook out a few slivers of ice, wrung the cloth out, and meticulously refilled it with cubes from behind the bar.

"Thanks," I said when he handed it back. I put it to my bruised flesh and sat very still. Snippets of conversation began to register.

"When Zack landed that kick in the second round, I thought he had him."

"Nah, man," said someone. "That just woke Gutierrez up, and he poured it on. Man, that guy's gonna be world champ someday."

"You did us all proud today, Zack," someone else said, slapping my back, which jolted me with fresh pain. "How about a drink?"

Esteban frowned and shook his head. "No, no, no. Zack don't drink. Zack never drinks."

The guy looked at Esteban and then at me. "Special Ed here for real? You work in a bar."

I shrugged, sending another wave of hurt cascading through my injured cranium. I moaned softly, and my mind drifted away again. No one bothered me for a few minutes, and my head finally stopped hammering so hard.

Esteban placed an envelope on the bar in front of me.

"Zack, look. A letter came for you."

I looked at it, puzzled. Only my friend Ben knew where I was, and he always phoned, never wrote. He was supposed to call later to find out how I'd done. We'd have a good laugh when I explained how badly I'd got my butt whipped.

I put down the cloth and picked up the envelope. There was my name, in spiky handwriting, with no return address and a postmark from North Carolina.

Since my arms felt tired and heavy from the pounding I'd taken, it took a fumbling minute to pull out a newspaper clipping and a folded sheet of paper. The clipping fell, and fluttered to the floor. Somebody reached down to pick it up while I tried to read what looked like a letter. Moisture from the bar had mottled the paper with large, wet blots.

"You dropped this," someone said. I waved him off, trying to concentrate on making sense of the letter. He spoke again. "Don't you know a guy named Benjamin Sterling?"

"Yeah, Ben's my best friend," I said. I put down the letter and turned in the direction of the voice, my head pounding in protest. "Is he on the phone?"

There was no answer, just a sudden, strange silence. The guy looked away, and thrust the clipping at someone else. That guy frowned while reading it, then looked up at me.

"What is it?" I asked.

A Darkened Room

Neither of them spoke. The second guy put the piece of paper on the bar, and they both silently slipped back into the crowd. Wondering at their strange behavior, I picked up the clipping. It was from the Press-Herald in Portland, Maine. It said that Benjamin Sterling, a cook at the Pine Haven resort, had died from a self-inflicted gunshot wound, after a brief period in the Portland hospital for food poisoning.

No. It wasn't true, couldn't be true. No way. It was some other Ben Sterling. "No, no," I rasped. It was a joke, a sick joke.

Someone put a hand on my shoulder. I shrugged it away, angry. I grabbed the letter from the bar. My hands were shaking as I read it:

Dear Zak,

We never got along but Ben always sed that we were the only two who mattered in his life. I rote to say how sorry I am about his dying. I still cant believe he done it. Shows you just never know. Thay called me from Main and buryed him in the city cimatarry. I woulda called you but dint have no number, just this address.

Maureen

P.S. I did love him, but we was just too differnt.

I felt cold inside, confused. I didn't believe it. What the hell was Ben's ex-wife up to? I read it again, and found myself trembling. My jaw was clenched so tight my teeth hurt. Killed himself? No damn way. I scanned the clipping again, trying to make sense of it, for Ben would never do that. Not ever.

I tried to stand, but dizziness forced me back onto the stool. People mumbled condolences, but their words slid off me like cold raindrops. I tuned them out. I needed a drink to push this away. My past came rushing back once more, after all the years of trying to forget. The floodwaters of memory swept in; I went under.

Some time later, the crowd was gone. Without people here, the room was too empty and still. It reminded me of the hollow ache inside.

Esteban stood staring at me, not moving. The pounding in my head had subsided to a dull ache, and the dizziness was gone. I wondered how long he and I had been like this.

I started breathing again. "Is Hernando upstairs?"

Esteban nodded, then shifted his eyes downward. "The bad man's with him."

"Raul?" I growled. "Did he push you again?"

"No. He only called me a stupid retard. It's okay."

"It's not okay!" I roared, slamming my hands to the bar and jumping up. The stool crashed to the floor, and Esteban backed away, looking terrified. I closed my eyes and ground my hands into my face. I couldn't stop shaking. I forced calm into my voice.

"I'm sorry, Esteban. I didn't mean to yell. Forget what he said. There's nothing wrong with you." I looked toward the back, to the stairs leading to Hernando's office. "He's just a bad man who enjoys hurting other people. And he has to stop."

I felt the old rage stir within me, a beast unchained and hungry. Something was going to happen. Something bad.

Dale T. Phillips

AFTERWORD

A Darkened Room is the sixth in the series about Zack Taylor, a man with many problems. He struggles to do better, but the deeds of his past weigh him down. When he tries to help others, he finds that doing good is a complicated matter, and unintended consequences force life-changing alterations.

There is much to think about for those who wish to peel back the layers. If not, just enjoy a good action yarn.

Should you be startled at certain anachronisms, it's because this book is set in the 1990's.

This is a work of fiction, and any resemblance to actual persons, living or dead, is purely coincidental.

Dale T. Phillips

ABOUT THE AUTHOR

A lifelong student of mysteries, Maine, and the martial arts, Dale T. Phillips has combined all of these into *A Darkened Room*. His travels and background allow him to paint a compelling picture of Zack Taylor, a man with a mission, but one at odds with himself and his new environment.

A longtime follower of mystery fiction, the author has crafted a hero in the mold of Travis McGee, Doc Ford, and John Cain, a moral man at heart who finds himself faced with difficult choices in a dangerous world. But Maine is different from the mean, big-city streets of New York, Boston, or L.A., and Zack must learn quickly if he is to survive.

Dale studied writing with Stephen King, and has published novels, over 70 short stories, collections, as well as poetry, articles, and non-fiction. He has appeared on stage, television, and in an independent feature film, *Throg*. He has also appeared on *Jeopardy* losing in a spectacular fashion. He co-wrote and acted in *The Nine*, a short political satire film. He has traveled to all 50 states, Mexico, Canada, and through Europe.

Dale T. Phillips

Connect Online:
Website: http://www.daletphillips.com
Blog: http://daletphillips.blogspot.com/
Facebook:
https://www.facebook.com/DaleTPhillips/
Twitter: DalePhillips2

Try these other works by Dale T. Phillips

Shadow of the Wendigo (Supernatural Thriller)

The Zack Taylor Mystery Series
A Memory of Grief
A Fall From Grace
A Shadow on the Wall
A Certain Slant of Light
A Sharp Medicine

Story Collections
Fables and Fantasies (Fantasy)
More Fables and Fantasies (Fantasy)

Crooked Paths (Mystery/Crime)
More Crooked Paths (Mystery/Crime)
The Last Crooked Paths (Mystery/Crime)
Strange Tales (Magic Realism, Paranormal)

Dale T. Phillips

Apocalypse Tango (Science Fiction)
Halls of Horror (Horror)
Jumble Sale (Different d Genres)
The Big Book of Genre Stories (Different Genres)

Non-fiction Career Help
How to Improve Your Interviewing Skills

With Other Authors
Rogue Wave: Best New England Crime Stories 2015
Red Dawn: Best New England Crime Stories 2016
Windward: Best New England Crime Stories 2017
Insanity Tales
Insanity Tales II: The Sense of Fear

Sign up for my newsletter to get special offers
http://www.daletphillips.com

Made in the
USA
Columbia, SC